RELENTLESS

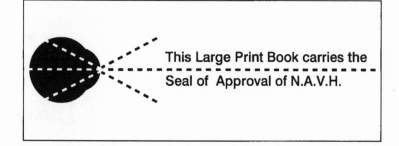

RELENTLESS

ED GORMAN

Thorndike Press • Waterville, Maine

Published in 2003 by arrangement with
The Berkley Publishing Group, a member of Penguin Group (USA) Inc.

Thorndike Press® Large Print Western.

The tree indicium is a trademark of Thorndike Press.

The text of this Large Print edition is unabridged.
Other aspects of the book may vary from the original edition.

Set in 16 pt. Plantin.

Printed in the United States on permanent paper.

Library of Congress Cataloging-in-Publication Data

Gorman, Edward.
    Relentless / Ed Gorman.
        p. cm.
    ISBN 0-7862-5595-1 (lg. print : hc : alk. paper)
    1. United States marshals — Fiction.   2. Colorado —
Fiction.   3. Large type books.   I. Title.
PS3557.O759R45 2003
    813'.54—dc21   2003050963

This is for
Sue Garvin

As the Founder/CEO of NAVH, the only national health agency solely devoted to those who, although not totally blind, have an eye disease which could lead to serious visual impairment, I am pleased to recognize Thorndike Press* as one of the leading publishers in the large print field.

Founded in 1954 in San Francisco to prepare large print textbooks for partially seeing children, NAVH became the pioneer and standard setting agency in the preparation of large type.

Today, those publishers who meet our standards carry the prestigious "Seal of Approval" indicating high quality large print. We are delighted that Thorndike Press is one of the publishers whose titles meet these standards. We are also pleased to recognize the significant contribution Thorndike Press is making in this important and growing field.

Lorraine H. Marchi, L.H.D.
Founder/CEO
NAVH

* Thorndike Press encompasses the following imprints: Thorndike, Wheeler, Walker and Large Print Press.

ONE

I always like to disappoint the young ones a little. Get some of that dime-novel nonsense out of their heads.

And so, when they raise their hands and ask me what a town marshal does all day long, I tell them that he sits in town council meetings, or tries to talk a teary woman into giving her drunken husband one more chance, or makes sure that everyone who is selling livestock within the town limits has been approved to do so. And so on. Boring stuff.

What they want to hear about is all the shoot-outs I get into. And all the wild Indians I have to drive away. And all the train robbers I round up. Lately, train robberies seem especially popular in dime novels — I know this because a couple of my deputies are always reading the damned things — and that's all kids want to hear about.

My hour of speaking to the kids in the one-story red-brick schoolhouse was just about coming to an end when the very pretty schoolmarm said, "We have time for one more question. Anybody have one more?"

They were getting ready for their midday break. There was a pail of milk next to the teacher's desk — the kids took turns bringing the milk — and the lunch packages and pails were lined up neatly under the section of the front wall that had been painted black to write on with chalk. This was a pay school, each student's parent paying a minimal fee. Next year this so-called plank school — because it was made from thick planks — would be converted to a public school. The tax assessment would pay not only for a blackboard, but for a lot more schoolbooks, too.

A pudgy twelve-year-old with a missing tooth raised his hand. "My pa says if you testify against Trent Webley, his old man'll have you run out of town. Is that true?"

The schoolmarm froze for a moment. Several of the kids shot the questioner accusatory looks. They knew it was a rude question to ask. But I didn't sense malice in the question. The kid was just curious.

I saw pity in the eyes of the slender red-haired schoolmarm. She knew all too well the history behind the kid's question. In addition to being the teacher here, Callie was also my wife. She was also the woman who'd educated me over the years. I hadn't been able to read very well when I'd met her. And I didn't have much interest in books or even magazines back then. But she'd changed all that.

"That's a good question." I smiled. "I can't honestly say I was expecting it, but I'll be happy to answer it." I looked around at all the faces. Smart, dumb, sweet, cunning, sad, bored, the typical mix of any classroom. I wished I'd had a school this nice to go to. I wished I'd had a teacher this pretty to daydream about. "Earlier you asked me who a town marshal has to fear most. Well, there's a simple answer to that. Sometimes, that's the people he works for. The citizens. Sometimes, they don't want you to carry out the law. Sometimes, they have good reasons for this. And sometimes, they have bad reasons. But if a town marshal's honest, he has to apply the law the same way to everybody."

"Even Paul Webley?" the kid said.

"Even Paul."

The kid grinned. "My dad likes you. But he says you got more guts than brains."

The children laughed.

"Well," I said, "I'm going to take that as a compliment."

If they were a little older and had a

firmer grasp of more subtle things, I'd tell them how a town marshal's most menacing enemy isn't the stray gunny or the ex-convict with a grudge, but the powerful people who run most towns. They're always wanting you to do them special favors. And when you can't or won't, they come after you. Usually they don't use guns or physical force of any kind. They use words, whispers, trying to undermine your authority in the eyes of the average citizen. If they're especially powerful, they'll have the town council, the same people who hired you, do their work for them. The council'll buy out any agreement you had with the town and send you on your way.

Callie stepped forward. She was a transplanted city girl and wore a lot of shirtwaist blouses and belted long skirts with her hair done in a bun. In Chicago they called this the "Gibson girl" look, the sort of style preferred by all the young women flocking to the cities as we approach the last decade of this century.

She held her brooch watch out for inspection. "It's such a nice day. How many children would like to eat lunch outdoors?"

Unanimous hand-waggling.

They got into a single long line, stumbling over each other as they did so, and when Callie gave the word the line, like a Chinese paper dragon, jerked its way outside.

"Sorry if Clete Browne's question embarrassed you."

The smell of October was warm and dusty through the lone open window. Chalk dust. Ink. Hair tonic to slick down the boys' hair; pretty-water, as they called it, to enhance the curls of the girls. I was all alone with the schoolmarm in this room of blackboard, globe, flag, and desk, and I wanted to kiss her, but I knew better. Even though we were married, one of the kids would see us, report us to his parents, and somebody would complain to his pastor or the newspaper editor. By the time the story had circulated all the way through town, we'd have been fornicating on the desk.

"It's what people are talking about," I said. "It's natural for a kid to bring it up."

She said, in her best cool voice, "You could always change your mind."

My voice wasn't cool at all. "I thought we'd settled that."

"It's just — If he'd shot you, that'd be one thing, Lane. But he didn't."

I shook my head. "Now you're sounding like his father. He only missed me because he was too drunk to hit me. The fact is, he shot at me with intent to kill. Bad enough if I was just a citizen. But I'm also a lawman. The law has to mean something, doesn't it?"

"You're getting a little pompous, Lane."

She walked to the window. Watched the children eat and play. Their voices ached with youth. Or maybe it was my hearing that their voices ached with youth — a youth and young manhood wasted on trail towns that needed simple laws enforced. I wasn't a gunny or a brave man. That's generally more dime-novel stuff. I was an administrator. I took over a town, chose five deputies who were family men, didn't drink or gamble or particularly enjoy a fight, gave them some training in the ways of law enforcement and some understanding of law, and put them to work. There was to be no dueling, no concealed weapons, no guns in town. I worked closely with the county attorney and the area judge. I help recruit qualified jury members and the court docket was dealt with swiftly. In all those years, I killed one man, and I wouldn't have killed him if he hadn't been so drunk that he fell into the path of my single wild shot. I used fines and county jails the way other lawmen used guns and clubs. The towns seemed generally appreciative of my work.

Three years ago, just before coming to Colorado, I went to a peace officers' seminar in Chicago. Callie was one of the young women who'd passed out leaflets and brochures at the function. This was summertime. Her teaching was over for three months. She was lovely but not quite fresh. Being a cynical lawman, I assumed there were things in her past she'd get around to telling me about someday. It wasn't anything I gave much thought to. I loved her in the slightly awkward way of a man who'd never had much success with women and who was just a tad bit afraid she'd someday walk out on me.

"You're mad," I said.

"No, I'm not."

"Sure, you are. You never say I'm being pompous unless you're mad."

She turned from the window to face me. "I like it here in Skylar, Lane. We have friends here, people who like us and respect us. Those are things I haven't had much in my life."

The past of hers I didn't know much of anything about, except that she'd spent most of her time teaching. But the pain in her voice and in her eyes said that there'd

13

been other things, too. Bad things.

She sighed. "I'm sorry, Lane. I'm not being fair. You're standing on principle, and I'm just being selfish."

"Don't make me more than I am, honey. I might reconsider this whole thing if I hadn't been the one he fired at. But I don't like the idea of somebody shooting at me and then having their rich daddy talk me out of pressing charges."

A couple of the kids had come to school on horseback. They'd left the animals ground-tied. Now the country kids were introducing the town kids to the mounts.

"I'm always afraid one of them's going to break his neck," she said. "Most of them don't know any more about horses than I did growing up in Chicago."

My railroad watch said it was time to get back to the office. "I'll see you at supper."

She took my hands. "I wish I could kiss you."

"Same here."

"Do the right thing, Lane. You usually do. I don't want to stand in the way. Testify against him this Thursday and if we have to leave town, we'll leave town. We're young enough to start over again."

I wouldn't have seen the envelope if I hadn't bumped my hip against her desk, knocking several books to the floor. When I bent to pick them up, I saw that she'd stuck a white business envelope between two of the books. THE ROYALTON HOTEL, CHICAGO'S FINEST was the imprinted return address. "Callie Morgan, Skylar, Colorado" was written on it in a broad masculine hand.

I would've asked her about it, but a kid let out a wail just then. Callie rushed to the door to see what was wrong.

I put the books back on the desk and pushed the envelope between two of them. For years I'd arrested men who got in jealous scraps over women. Not having a woman of my own, I'd always felt a little bit smug about jealousy. As if it wouldn't ever happen to me. But now that I had a woman of my own, it happened to me all the time. Men who stared at her a little too long; men who asked her to dance one time too many at social events; even the stray man who flirted with her from time to time. One of the few things she'd told me about her past was that she'd had a number of jealous suitors and that jealousy made her angry. She was always faithful, she'd told me, and never encouraged men to approach her in any untoward way. She'd warned me that I'd be best off keeping jealous thoughts to myself.

What I wanted to do was open the envelope, which she'd already done, and read the letter. It might be a business letter, but I doubted it.

Some piece of her past had returned. No doubt about that. A man. A former suitor? One of the jealous ones?

I put my hand out and touched the edge of the envelope. She was busy outside. She'd stopped the wailing. Now she'd have to find out what was going on.

So easy to give the letter a quick read. But what if I read words that I'd never again be able to get out of my mind? What if I read words that somehow altered our marriage forever? What if she'd been writing an old beau on a steady basis and I hadn't found out about it till now?

From the doorway, she said, "Are you all right?"

She was silhouetted in the door frame, blue sky and snow-peaked mountains behind her. She walked up to me. I didn't move. I saw her look at me and then at the books on the edge of her desk. And the edge of the white envelope jutting out like a sin exposed.

Something changed in her gray eyes when she saw the envelope. She must have realized that I'd seen it, too.

"Maybe we should have a talk tonight," she said softly.

I shrugged. "If you think so." I didn't want to say anything more than was absolutely necessary. Sometimes words just speak themselves, and they're always words you want to take back.

She took my hands in hers again. "The one thing we agreed to was that we'd always trust each other, Lane. I need you to trust me now."

Two girls burst through the door. One of them held her head tilted far back. "She's got a nosebleed, Mrs. Morgan. Judy punched her right in the face."

I headed back to the office.

TWO

You know how it is when you first start a job. Everybody eager to please you and you eager to please them. The only thing that gave them pause the day I took the job was a request for $500 in office furniture. "Hell, Lane, we've got a desk and a chair there." But I wanted more than a desk and chair. I wanted the curtain-top style of desk I was used to working at, and two standard-style desks for my senior day deputy and my senior night deputy. I wanted a cork bulletin board for wanted posters that would be updated once a week, and I wanted a plain five-shelf oak $4 bookcase that I'd load up with books and magazines pertaining to modern law enforcement. I wanted a good coffeepot and a small box-style stove that would fit unobtrusively in the corner. All this got the inevitable laughs among the council members and all the people they told, but the day it was all put together and unveiled, the town saw something it had never seen before: a professional town marshal's office.

The same cleaning woman who took care of the four-cell jail on the second floor also dusted and tidied up the office every morning, too.

When I walked in, I smelled sweet-scented furniture polish. Solid Tom Ryan, my senior day deputy, was at his desk doing paperwork, the scourge of all peace officers who take their job seriously. Tom Ryan was solid of body and solid of mind, one of the best deputies I'd ever had. Some people found the big towhead a little cool, but that was just because he didn't allow himself the luxury of running his mouth. He sized up a person or a situation before he said or did anything. He had one problem. He'd bought a small ranch on the edge of town when he was younger. He lost money on it every year. He was a terrible rancher. Now the bank was going to take the paper back on it. He was always looking for new ways to raise money to pay off the ranch. He was so damned sensible otherwise. Every man and every woman has something that makes them a little crazy. That was Tom and his ranch.

"How'd it go at school, Lane?"

"They wanted to know how many train robbers I'd killed lately."

He laughed. "That's what they wanted to know the time your wife invited me out there."

"Any business?" I said, sitting down at my desk. The night sheet was written in neat longhand for me to see. The usual. Two drunk-and-disorderlies. Another drunk who smashed out a saloon window with a rock after the barkeep cut him off. Nothing notable.

"You want to go see Mrs. Daly or you want me to do it?"

I shook my head. "Poor old lady. But at least I have some good news for her."

Mrs. Daly was a widower a scam artist had managed to swindle $500 from. He'd convinced her that he had to sell the family jewels, literally, in order to save the family manse near Denver. He brought a forged letter with him from a local banker whose name she recognized. She gave him the $500. I caught the bastard four days later in a whorehouse where the madam had summoned me. He'd gone through all the money and was now drunkenly demanding free merchandise.

Leaving Lucy Daly with a tax bill she couldn't pay and hadn't paid for nearly three years now.

"What's the good news?"

"I got the county assessor to re-appraise her property. He cut the tax assessment in half and agreed to accept quarterly payment for the next four years."

"Lucy's going to be saying a whole lot of masses for you, Lane."

"I could use them." Lucy probably would, too. She was a devout woman.

"Any prisoners upstairs?"

He shook his head. "I got them over to the courthouse. The judge fined all three of them and let them go."

"Good. I want to open the doors and windows up there and air the place out."

"You sure do run an accommodating jail. Clean, good food, the guard gets fined if he gets too rough."

The slight sarcasm in his voice edged upward when he came to the last part, about the guards being fined. Very few townspeople, including my deputies, liked my idea of running a clean, safe jail. They especially didn't understand why I'd fine a guard who got too rough with a prisoner. But to me, it was all part of being a professional lawman. There's nothing in the law that gives a peace officer the right to brutalize a prisoner. On the other hand, I have a rule that says that any prisoner who lies about a guard hurting him gets the exact punishment he lied about. If he said the guard hit him three times in the face, he gets hit by that guard three times in the face.

"Oh, I got Conroy on the stage," Ryan said. "He gave me quite a tussle. Didn't want to leave. Seems he liked our little town. Drew a nice little crowd when he started fighting me in front of the stage."

"Thanks, Tom." Conroy was a confidence man who'd just started working Skylar. We managed to catch him fast. And get him on a stage and get him out of town.

I hadn't had time to sort through the mail stacked on the far right corner of my otherwise clean desk.

Seeing the mail there, I thought of the envelope Callie had stuck between two of her schoolbooks. The letter from the Royalton Hotel in Chicago. I wondered what she was going to tell me tonight. Something I probably didn't want to hear, to know. Something that just might alter our marriage forever.

I slogged through the mail. There was a time when I thought illiterate people were stupid. I'd graduated high school myself. But I'd been out on the street long enough now to know that the opposite was true. Illiterate people could be awfully smart and literate people could be awfully dumb. A lot of the letters of complaint I get are in a kind of pidgin English. I'd gotten pretty good at translating. What all these letters came down to was that they wanted help. Most of them were immigrants, Germans, Irish, a handful of Jews and Swedes, who were finding America less accommodating than they'd expected. The problems they described weren't monumental, but it was easy to see that they were ongoing and frustrating problems — mostly having to do with getting hired and getting a line of credit and finding a neighborhood that would accept them — and so I helped any way I could. I usually went to the party they were having trouble with and pleaded the immigrants' case for them. And got some satisfaction. If you approach most people reasonably, they'll respond reasonably.

I was halfway through the pile when Tom Ryan said, "That Hastings kid is still looking for you. He's been here a week now."

"Aw, shit," I said.

"Says he wants to 'fight the man who outdrew Sansom.' "

"I didn't outdraw Sansom. He was so damned drunk he fell into the path of my bullet."

Tom grinned. "Well, that still hasn't stopped people from turning you into a legend. Peace-loving lawman kills notorious killer. That kind of thing."

"And Hastings traveled all the way from Mesa, Arizona, to fight me?"

"That's what I'm told. I guess some yellowback writer said if he managed to kill you, he'd write a book about him."

"He came all the way up here because of that?"

"He's nineteen, Lane. You know how you are when you're nineteen."

"Thank God I was never nineteen that way. I wasn't any wizard, but at least I knew better than to take the word of some asshole who wrote yellowbacks for a living. Where's he staying?"

Tom looked surprised. "You aren't going to fight him, are you?"

"No, but I'm going to have a little talk with him before I swing out and see Lucy Daly with the good news."

"He's at the Excelsior."

I got through the mail before I left. Most of it went into the wastebasket. I stood up, grabbed my hat, and said, "I'll be back around three."

"You need any help?"

"Last time I looked, Lucy Daly weighed about eighty pounds and was blind in one eye. I think I can whip her."

"Very funny. I mean with the punk."

"Thanks for the offer, Tom. But I think I can handle him, too."

Perry Dolan, the day clerk at the Excelsior Hotel, nodded when he saw me approach the front desk. "You look pretty serious this morning, Marshal. You must've lost some money in one of Gunderson's card games upstairs."

I smiled. "I'm smart enough to stay out of those, believe me."

"You looking for somebody?"

"You got a kid named Ned Hastings."

"I figured that's what it was about. He ran his mouth all over town last night. We had to carry him up to his room." Dolan had a round, friendly face. "He ain't in no danger of becomin' a beloved figure."

"He's going to fight me?"

"That's what he tells everybody."

I shook my head. "I've got a few other things on my mind. I need to settle this fast."

"He's up there if you want him."

"Give me the extra key."

He did.

"You going to shoot him, Marshal?"

I smiled. "Sure, Perry. Shoot him in his sleep. That's pretty much what I'm known for, isn't it?"

He laughed. "You know what I mean. You going to force him into a gunfight?"

"Can you remember any gunfight happening in this town since I became marshal?"

He hesitated. "Say, that's right."

"And there won't be any this time either." I nodded to his coffeepot. "How about giving me a cup of that to take upstairs?"

He looked puzzled, then shrugged and got the coffee.

The hotel was pretty much empty for the day. The drummers who stayed here would all be out drumming, and the new folks hadn't yet arrived for tonight. An orange tomcat sat at the top of the landing, his fur being bombarded by the dust motes in the golden sun streaming through the window.

Ned Hastings was snoring loudly enough to rattle the door. I let myself in. He looked like every would-be tinhorn gunny I'd ever seen. He'd been so drunk he slept in his clothes. Fancy leather cowboy boots. Fancy white six-guns riding in a fancy black holster rig. A fancy black vest that would have looked nicer against the white shirt if the white shirt hadn't been soiled with vomit, beer, and blood. His nose was bloody. Drunks were always hurting themselves. Or letting other people hurt them.

A carpetbag sat in the corner. On the bureau was a framed reverent photograph of a striking young woman who bore a definite resemblance to Ned. Either his sister or his mother in her youth. Hard to say.

I didn't have any trouble with his sixguns. He went right on snoring. Every once in a while he farted. The room was starting to suffocate me with its hothouse odors.

When I finished with his guns, I grabbed his hair and yanked him to his feet. He cursed, managed to get his eyes open, cursed some more, tried to swing at me, and made a choking sound convincing enough so that I let him go long enough to throw up in the chamber pot.

While he was wiping off his mouth with the back of his hand, I handed him the steaming cup of coffee. He needed a shave, a bath, and a little humility.

"Who the hell are you?"

"The first clue," I said, tapping my marshal's star, "is that I'm the law."

"I shoot somebody last night?"

"You probably tried."

He sipped some coffee, made a face. "This tastes like shit."

"Drink it anyway."

He was gradually coming awake. He

27

glanced at the bureau. "What're those?"

"Bullets."

"I know they're bullets." Then he looked down at his guns and said, "Hey, those're my bullets."

"That's right." I took out my Colt. Held my hand out, palm up, emptied my own gun. Set the six bullets on the bureau next to his. "And this is my gun."

"What the hell you trying to prove anyway?"

"That you'd be crazy to fight me."

"You killin' Sansom doesn't scare me none."

"I didn't kill Sansom. Sansom killed Sansom. He was so drunk, he fell into my bullet. He stumbled at the exact moment my bullet was going past him. It was a warning shot was all."

He touched a trembling hand to his forehead. This was probably too much for him to grasp in the first hot, dehydrated, spooky moments of hangover. "So what's the point of empty guns?"

"When you finish your coffee, I want you to draw down on me."

"With an empty gun?"

"That's right."

"Why would I do that?"

"Because if there were bullets in our

guns, I'd kill you. And I don't think your mom or your sister or whoever's in that picture over there would appreciate that."

He grinned with bad teeth, his wisp of a mustache looking like spider legs on his upper lip. "You gonna teach me a lesson, huh?"

"I'm going to try. And if you're smart, it's a lesson you'll remember."

"This is damned silly. People'll laugh when they hear it."

"It's not any sillier than fighting with bullets. Most things can be worked out by talking them through. Unless the people involved are drunk or stupid. Now put that damned coffee down and draw on me."

He made a big show of starting to feint to the left, setting his coffee on the bureau. But what he did, of course, was angle to the right and grab one of his guns. Even with his momentary head start, my Colt was clear and pointing right at his chest before his had even cleared leather.

"You sonofabitch."

"You'd be dead, kid."

"You got me at a bad time. I'm still sorta drunk from last night."

"Kid, I spent six years in the Army. Dullest job I ever had. We mostly pulled sentry duty. But instead of walking post,

29

we played a lot of cards and worked on our draws. I was about your age. I got pretty fast, but I was slow compared to a lot of the other soldiers. There never was a Wild West, kid. Not in the way you think there was. There were a lot of drunken back-shooters and ambushers and men like Sansom who were so drunk they stumbled into bullets. But actual gunfights between sober men? The old duels in the South, those were gunfights. And they had strict rules. But you're trying to live out some bullshit you read about in a dime novel. That's up to you, kid. But you're not going to live it out in this town, you understand? There's a train at three and a stage at four. Take your choice. Be on one or the other."

"I rode in with my own horse."

"Tough shit. Train or stage. I'll have deputies at each depot to make sure you get on board."

"What if I don't?"

"Then you go to jail."

"For what?"

I smiled. "I'm not sure yet. But I've got a pretty good mind when it comes to thinking up ways to keep youngsters like you in jail."

He did it. I expected it. He did it and I did it, and I beat him to it even faster than I had before.

"And in every town you go to, kid, there'll be ten men even faster than I am. And they won't be gunnies, they'll just be average citizens all settled down and married. They do their fast draws at family reunions and picnics to show off to the grandkids. They wouldn't get into a gun-fight any more than you'd try to jump off a mountain and fly. That fast-draw stuff is strictly for yellowbacks, kid. And you'd better learn that before it's too late."

He threw a lot of dirty words at the door I was pulling closed behind me. I hoped he'd take the train or the stage. I didn't like him. I didn't want him in my jail.

Perry Dolan looked up as I walked over to his front desk. "You take care of him, Marshal?"

"Shot him four times in his sleep. In the back."

"You ever gonna let me forget that?"

I laughed. "Not anytime soon."

"Hey," he said, "what's this?"

He hefted a large envelope on the palm of his hand, then held it up for me to see. It had my name on it. No stamp, no other markings.

"Where'd this come from?" I said.

"I don't know. I had to step down the hall a minute. I guess somebody must've

31

put it here when I was gone. Anyway, here you go."

I took the envelope with me. I headed for the livery. I was looking forward to giving Lucy Daly the good news.

About a block from the livery I opened the envelope and peeked inside. I didn't have any time to give it a proper count, but a rough guess put the value of all those greenbacks inside at somewhere around $10,000.

There was a simple card with a type-written note on it.

FROM A FRIEND

THREE

The envelope rode in my saddlebags all the way out to Lucy Daly's and back. Even when Lucy was hugging me and making me eat one of her locally famous muffins, all I could think about was what that envelope meant. She got a little teary at the end, Lucy did, so thankful that I'd been able to strike a deal with the tax assessor, who'd come up with some alternative way to assess her. She looked worn and sweet and lonely standing there on the porch of her faded little ranch house. She made me wonder about my own folks back in Nebraska. I really did need to see them soon. I wasn't getting any younger and they sure as hell weren't either.

My first hour back in town was taken up with a squabble between Larry Carstairs, who runs one of the two general stores, and his competitor Max Barlow, who runs the other one. They'd gotten into a fistfight right in the middle of the street over something that one of them allegedly said about the other. The person who'd started the fight was one Kenneth T. Blaine, a haberdasher who loved to start trouble. When he couldn't do it by passing along legitimate gossip, he just made it up.

Now, a fistfight isn't usually a big problem for a peace officer. No guns, no knives, just fists. You angle yourself in between the fighters and give each of them a shove in the opposite direction.

But there's something you have to know about Carstairs and Barlow. Larry's sixty-eight, and Max is seventy-one. Larry has a heart condition, and Barlow has asthma so bad you can hear him coming a block away.

There is always an element of folks who'll turn out for any kind of fight — dogs, cats, kids, doesn't matter as long as there's combat of some sort.

But this was ridiculous, two old coots swinging wild like this, either one of them perfectly capable of dropping dead on the spot.

I didn't give either of them a shove. I was afraid to. What I did was get my arms around each of their necks and start moving them toward the shade of our town park. We've got some nice elms standing over park benches there.

I didn't pay any attention to what they were saying. I just told somebody to run and get their wives.

With that suggestion, both men quit their angry babbling.

"What you want to go and do that for?" Larry said.

"We can settle this our ownselves," Max said.

"Yeah, you were doing a fine job of it," I said. "The temperature's somewhere in the high eighties, you both have serious medical conditions, and between you you're going on two hundred years old. Yeah, you were doing a damn fine job of it, all right."

"She's gonna kick my ass clear into the next county, Sheriff," Larry said, sounding like a scared little kid.

"Good," I said. "Maybe next time, you'll keep that in mind."

"She won't bake me a pie for two weeks," Max said. "That's how she always punishes me."

"I just wish that damned Kenny Blaine hadn't told me what you said about me," Larry said.

"That's what I was tryin' to tell you," Larry said. "I didn't say it. And if I wanted to say it, I sure as hell wouldn't say it to Kenny Blaine, who'd go right straight to you and tell you I said it."

I left it to their wives to sort through it all.

I was just finishing up my mail when he came in. The sudden silence was what made me look up. Tom had been talking to another deputy about an upcoming court trial when the door opened. And then they stopped talking.

I looked up to see what could possibly cause them to just quit speaking. And there in the doorway stood my answer.

You think of important men as exuding their importance. Something lionlike in their look or manner or gait. You don't think of them as small, slight men with small, slight voices and nervous little mannerisms. It was said that Paul could fill your ashtray with his fingernails. He was always anxiously chewing on them and spitting them out. This wasn't to say that he wasn't capable of violence. But he ordered it, he didn't participate in it.

He said, "I wondered if we might speak somewhere alone, Marshal."

Tom said, "Time for our break anyway, Lane. Why don't we head down the street." Tom always knew how to handle things.

"Sure."

They left.

"I'm sorry to interrupt your day this way, Marshal."

"Why don't you sit down, Paul?"

He sat down. He wore a cheap suit, had a cheap haircut, and smoked a cheap little corncob pipe. He couldn't have weighed more than one-thirty or topped five-five. How he'd produced his strapping, belligerent son had long been a subject of comic speculation.

He bit a nail and said, "Did you get my package?"

"Yes, I did, Paul."

"That's a serious offer."

"I know that."

"I'm just trying to spare you and the town some trouble."

"I know that, too, Paul."

"This has changed him, Marshal."

"I see."

"I know that sounds like something any father would say, but it really has changed him. Made Trent see the kind of young man he's turning into. Throwing his weight around and bullying people and everything." He hesitated. Bit on a nail. "It's kind of funny."

"Oh?"

"My father was a big, burly man just like Trent is. He was always sorry that I didn't turn out more like him. I suppose he figured it took a big man to oversee everything he'd built up for himself — two short-line railroads, a big cattle spread, three different factories right here in town, half-dozen banks — he didn't think I could ever handle it all. I just wish he could've lived to see me triple everything he did. These days a man needs brains, not brawn."

"I agree."

Another gnaw on his nail. He spat the residue precisely into my empty ashtray. "He's a throwback, Trent is. I'm working on him, Marshal. I really am. I want him to make something of himself before it's too late."

I hated to say it, but I had to. I believed Paul's contrition and humility. But he had to look at the facts. "He tried to kill me, Paul. I'm the law here. There are half-dozen witnesses to what he did."

He cleared his throat. "They're not going to testify."

There was always a point in any conversation with Paul when you had to take a closer look at him. And when you did take a second look, you saw the big strapping soul of his reflected in his eyes. He might not have his daddy's body, but he sure did have his daddy's heart and spirit. He would do anything to have his way.

"I see," I said.

"They're good citizens, Marshal, that's all. They don't think a trial would be good for the town. People would take sides, argue. They love this town as much as I do." He paused. "And as much as you do, Marshal. Because I know you love this town."

We were now officially in bullshit land. He'd come in here sincerely enough, a father doing his desperate best to save his son from a prison stint. But now he was all calculation and oil, trying to smooth me into agreeing with him. There was an implicit threat in all this, of course. In a very real sense, he ran this town.

"I'm hoping you'll keep that envelope, Marshal."

"Can't."

"Why not?"

"First, because it's a bribe. And if I accepted it, then I'd be just as guilty as you are right now. Second, because I still plan to testify tomorrow. Third, because I meant what I said. Even if I did want to back down, I couldn't. People saw him try to kill me. I admit he was drunk. And I admit he probably does regret doing it, if only because he knows he's in trouble now. But how the hell can I claim to be an impartial lawman if I let him get away with it?

I'm in just as much a fix here as you and your boy are, Paul."

"You're not the one who'll have to go to prison."

I sighed. "Look, Paul, the county attorney wants to go ahead with this. He feels the same way I do. We don't have any choice. But I talked to him yesterday and he's agreed to recommend to the judge that we go easy on this. What it'll come down to is he drops the charges to drunk-and-disorderly, resisting arrest, and carrying a firearm in the city. He'll give him six months in county jail and a three-year probation. Now, Trent can sure as hell live with that."

"Do you know what my father would do if he knew his grandson was being sent to jail, even for six months?"

"Your father's dead, Paul."

"But his name isn't. His heritage isn't. We built this region, Marshal. It was my father's capital that got everything going out here."

This was the only part of the conversation that surprised me. I'd expected him to plead like a father, I'd expected him to threaten like a Webley, but I hadn't expected him to invoke some mythical, mystical "heritage" that sounded vaguely like the legend of King Arthur. Maybe there was a magical sword somewhere in the Webley family.

Then: "Every town marshal before you cooperated with me, Lane. And I took care of them. They all retired with nice little bank accounts because of me. And if you won't cooperate with me, maybe the man who replaces you will."

I just shook my head. It wasn't a threat worth responding to. "I thought you'd be happy to hear what the county attorney came up with, Paul."

He stood up. I adjusted my evaluation of his height downward. Five-four. A kid with graying hair and wattles.

He slid it out from inside his jacket. It was a day for envelopes bearing all sorts of ominous news. A mysterious friend from my wife's past. A pack containing ten thousand dollars. And now what would this be?

We traded envelopes.

He picked up the ten thousand I pushed back at him, and while he was doing that, I checked out the envelope he pushed at me.

It wasn't addressed to anybody, but it had a familiar business name on the upper left-hand corner.

ROYALTON HOTEL
Chicago, Illinois

"There're some interesting things in there, Marshal. One day I got to worrying about you and your wife. Just curious. You know how people get. So I hired the Pinkertons to check you two out. You checked out pretty well, Marshal. A lot of people have a lot of respect for you." He hesitated, enjoying himself. "But your wife — and I'm sure she's a fine woman — well, why don't you read some of the things in there and see if you still want to testify tomorrow. I'm staying in town tonight at the hotel. I'll be glad to talk any time you want to."

And with that, he was gone.

I went to the window and watched him board his fancy buggy. His wife Laura waited there with fragile serenity. She was a treasure he'd brought back from the East. It was rumored that she was subject to serious mental lapses and had been in and out of asylums for much of her life. There were also rumors that she'd grown restless in Skylar. But there are always rumors about rich women, especially if they're as elegantly icy as Laura Webley.

FOUR

I put the letter in the drawer and left it there the rest of the afternoon. I was afraid if I read it I wouldn't get any work done.

A federal marshal had a train layover, so he stopped in to kill some time. We'd known each other slightly over the years but hadn't ever become friends, and that was obvious in the strained nature of our conversation.

After he left, a man from the livery came up and said he'd just had a horse come in bearing the brand that I'd alerted him to. A dozen of the horses had been rustled, nice roans that would bring a good price. He said the man who'd brought it in was now over at one of our more popular saloons.

I was grateful for activity. I locked my desk and left.

This was another one of those incidents that would disappoint the kids. In dime novels there'd be a shoot-out and law and order would prevail. Well, law and order did prevail, but not because of any shoot-out.

43

The rider, who looked barely old enough to get served, sat in the back of the saloon with a sudsy beer in hand talking to a tired-looking town drunk. I shooed the drunk away and sat down.

The kid looked at me and said, "Dammit, I should've known better."

"Better than what?"

"Ride that horse in here. With that brand still on it."

"Yeah, I guess you should've."

"But I had to see a doctor."

"How come?"

"This stitch in my stomach." He showed me where it was. "Hurts like hell and won't go away."

"You still got your appendix?"

"My what?"

"Your appendix."

"What's appendix mean?"

I told him. "That sounds like what it is," I said.

"No way am I gonna let him operate. I heard about them operations. How they go, I mean. Cuttin' you with a knife'n all. No way."

"You could die if you don't get it out."

"Die? From what?"

"Infection. You think you're in pain now, wait till it gets infected."

He was scared. He was a kid and probably a good ways from home and scared, and I didn't blame him at all. He looked up at me. "You gonna arrest me?"

"I have to."

"The rustlin', it was Walt's idea."

"Walt Crimmins?"

"Yeah. You heard of him?"

"I thought he was rustling up in Montana."

"He's got a gal somewhere near Denver. So we came down here." He grimaced. "You know the doctor here?"

"There are two of them. A woman and a man."

"A woman doctor?" he said. "I heard of that before, but I'd rather see the man, I guess. Especially if I have to take my pants off. I'd feel funny if I had to take my pants off in front of a woman and all." Then: "I just stopped in here to get a little courage." He nodded to his beer. Then: "How much time you think I'll have to do?"

"You cooperate, you help catch Crimmins, not too much. You ever been in trouble before?"

"I busted out some windows the night my dad died. I was pretty drunk. I was only ten. He died and they took him away — he had cholera — and I finished off his

45

last pint of whiskey and then I went to town and started smashin' out windows of stores. I couldn't even tell you why I done it. But the sheriff, he arrested me."

"That's the only time?"

"Pretty much."

"That'll help with the judge. Just that one arrest. And there were extenuating circumstances."

"What's that mean?"

"Means you were just a kid and that your dad had died and maybe you weren't quite right in the head."

"Some folks always says I'm never right in the head."

"I wouldn't mention that to the judge."

"I'm not crazy, if that's what you're thinkin'."

"I didn't say you were."

"I'm just a little high-strung. That's what my ma said was the only thing wrong with me, whatever them other people said. That I was just a little high-strung was all."

I took him over to the doctor, and the doctor examined him and said that the kid's appendix had to come out, and the kid broke down right there. Nothing big and dramatic. Just silent tears and real fear on the face.

Long shadows. That aching melancholy

of day's end. Kids scurrying home for supper. Merchants locking their doors. The barber taking in the wooden Indian he keeps outside on the boardwalk. The priest climbing the tower to ring the bell that only deepens the melancholy of the moment.

I sat in my office. My desk was still locked, the letter inside.

Deke Newton came in right at five, ready to take over for the night. Deke is part-Cherokee and part-Irish. He was an Army scout for a little over a decade before settling in with a wife and four kids, one of which always seems to be sick. He's quiet, reliable, quick as a snake. He isn't much for guns, which I'm happy about, but he knows various jabs and holds that can slam a man to the ground in seconds. He isn't anybody I'd ever care to fight. He wears dark suits, looks like a middle-aged businessman except for his shiny dark hair, and sports a badge that is always polished to a perfect gleam.

He got himself some coffee, sat down at his desk and went through the docket to see what kind of activity we'd had today, and then said, "You all right, Lane?"

"Yeah."

I couldn't take my eyes from the desk

drawer that held the letter.

He obviously sensed something wrong, but didn't push it. He wouldn't. Not his style. He stood up and grabbed the jail keys and did his first check of the cells.

By the time he was back, I had the letter shoved down in my jacket.

"Anything I should know about tonight?" he said.

"Well, I'm told there'll be a couple of night raiders coming in to lynch the night marshal, but other than that things look to be pretty quiet."

He grinned. "Why don't you hang around for a while? Maybe they'll think you're the night marshal. I've got six mouths to feed."

"Six? Your wife and five kids?"

"I don't need to eat?"

"I guess that's a fair point."

It was a little strained, and he knew it and I knew it, but strained was better than sulking, which is what I'd been doing when he came in.

"Only thing that happened was that Paul came to see me."

His eyes narrowed. "That must've been something."

"He hasn't changed any. Wants me to drop the charges — or just not show up to testify."

He paused before speaking, his features sharp in the darkening room. "Lot of people want you to back off, Lane."

"That include you, Deke?"

"You know better than that."

I put my hand out. We shook. "Thanks. I needed to hear that."

"Don't let him spook you, Lane. He's a little shit, but that's the one thing he's good at. I've been in this town a lot longer than you have, and I've learned one thing — Paul knows how to get his way without ever landing a single punch or firing a single shot."

I thought of the letter in my pocket. "Yeah, he sure does."

Win Evans came in. He was the junior night deputy, a former farmhand who is a big gentle bear until you push him a single inch across his private line. Then he's not so gentle at all. He's especially helpful on weekends when the youngsters take over the saloons. Deke and Win together are one hell of a formidable force. Perfect for the night watch.

I went out, walked over to the park, and sat down next to the Civil War memorial depicting one soldier carrying a wounded soldier on his back. My pop had been in the war. He screamed about it a lot in his sleep. I can still hear my mother shushing him, holding him, wrenching him from his nightmares so she could soothe him. It must've been a hell of a thing for him to see. It must've been a hell of a thing for anybody to see.

I took the letter out, and was about to open it and read it when I saw him across the street, watching me. I slid the letter back into my jacket. We stared at each other for a time, and then he started across to me, having to pause in the middle of the street to let a surrey go by.

He smelled of heat and sweat and barbershop oil. I was told he'd been sober since it had all happened, and I had to say I was impressed.

He put his hand out, clearly uncertain if I'd shake it. I shook it.

"I guess my dad was in to see you."

"Yeah, he was, Trent."

"He says you're still pretty pissed off at me."

"It isn't a matter of being pissed off, Trent. It's a matter of the law."

"Well, sometimes you can get around the law. If you really want to, I mean."

His sport was football and he was good at it. Hard to believe he'd been sired by Paul. The shoulders spanned a good four feet, the hands were powerful enough to put a dent in a surface of iron, and the legs were fast enough to outdistance a trained runner. He had dark, curly hair, blunt blue eyes, and a smile that made you like him unless you knew him.

I didn't think he was a bad kid, just an unlucky one. He was one of those people who couldn't hold his liquor. Later on, he'd have serious problems with the bottle — blackouts, hallucinations, maybe even a fatally damaged liver. But for now what he did was go somewhat insane whenever he went on one of his sporadic binges.

I'm no patron saint of lawmen. I live and work in a very political context. All peace officers do. I'd given him a lot of room because he was Paul's twenty-two-year-old son. He'd been in fights, he'd smashed up saloons, he'd even, if you wanted to get technical, stolen a horse. I always managed to handle these things. But the night he fired a Winchester at me — and it wasn't just shooting to make some noise, he deliberately aimed at my head — I didn't have any choice but to arrest him and charge him with attempted murder.

"I've already let you get around the law, Trent. Several times, in fact."

You could sense his disappointment. I

suppose he'd hoped that by coming over here and bowing and scraping a little, I might change my mind.

"I'm really sorry about what I did, Marshal."

"You know what? I believe you. That's why — and I sure hope your dad told you this — I've worked out a way so that you get minimum jail time. Hell, you could have served eight, nine years on this, Trent. You'll get six months at most. The rest will be probation."

He got mad. He didn't want to get mad. He knew he shouldn't get mad. But he couldn't help himself. "That isn't what I want and it sure as hell isn't what my dad wants, Marshal." He visibly forced himself to calm down. He sighed. "C'mon, Marshal, put yourself in our position for just a minute. That's all we're asking you to do. We're an important family in the valley. Maybe the most important. I know that sounds arrogant to say, but it's true. It just wouldn't look right for a Webley to go to jail. Even for six months."

Now it was my turn to sigh. "It's the best I can do, Trent. I'm sorry. I really am."

The anger was back. But this was cold anger. "My dad said he gave you a letter."

"Yes, he did."

"Well, I came over here hoping he wouldn't have to do anything about that letter. But I'll tell you — now we won't have any choice." The eyes were harsh. "I guess it's time everybody in this town heard the truth about that wife of yours."

He turned and walked away.

FIVE

She wasn't home.

Originally, our place was a cabin by the river. But a new roof and some white paint and a lot of vines crawling up the front and sides gave it the look of a cottage by a brook, a New England kind of feel that Callie wanted.

Conner, our collie, came to greet me, all long lapping tongue and quick jumps up to be petted. Sometimes during a long and difficult day, after I've thought how nice it will be to see Callie again, I think of old Conner. He's like the kid we've never been able to produce for some reason.

But Conner wasn't enough tonight.

All the way home — we live on the northeast edge of the town limits — I thought of what I'd say to Callie. How I'd approach the subject of the letter and its contents. I wouldn't be accusatory; I wouldn't be self-righteous; and I'd try very hard not to be pompous, something peace officers can do without knowing it. I'd ask her for the simple truth. And I'd take her word for what she said.

Just outside the open doorway I could hear the crickets and the night birds and the lonely call of coyotes. I poured myself a shot of bourbon and carried it out to the front stoop. Conner sat next to me on the step.

I had a lot of ideas where she might be, and all of them involved the same person. The man in the newspaper articles; the man on the WANTED poster. I wondered what her envelope had contained. Pretty much the same thing, I imagined.

Paul had been smart about it. If he couldn't get to me, maybe he could get to her. So give us both envelopes. And then give me one final chance to change my mind by having Trent come over and apologize and sound reasonable as all hell, until he realized that I wasn't going to change my mind.

I wondered how they'd spread the word. It wouldn't be anything as obvious as talking to the newspaper editor. He was a friend of mine and as much as he feared Webley, he wouldn't consent to any gossip-mongering in his weekly.

The town council would be his best opportunity. Under the guise of wanting to keep them apprised of their lawman's past, he could say, *This is the sort of woman he married. Is this the kind of man we want wearing our marshal's badge?*

It would be an obvious way to discredit me, to shift the trial tomorrow away from his boy and make it a trial about me. He'd be sure the jury heard the whispers before they were seated. And he'd be sure that they all knew how appreciative he'd be if they failed to convict his son. Trent would walk free and my reputation would be destroyed.

After an hour or so, the first stars gleaming in the clear night sky, I went inside and sliced off two pieces of bread and spread them with butter and jam, and sat down and had the sort of meal I used to enjoy when I was a kid.

I took the time, as I often did, to see how well she'd fixed up the cabin, everything from the bright cotton material that hid the open shelves that were packed with canned goods, to the crisp white curtains, to the colorful quilt she'd made for our bed, to the pie safe she'd constructed herself from wood and tin scraps, the safe plenty tight to store fresh food and pies in. She always laughed and said she wanted to make our home look as much like New England as possible.

I felt so many things and yet I felt — nothing. There was a deadness inside me. I'm not ashamed to say that I'm one of those men who cry sometimes when they're particularly frustrated or angry. Tears would have been a relief. But tears wouldn't come. There was just this emptiness — this coldness — that I knew foreshadowed a great rage. It was one thing for Webley to make a move on me. That was part of the game powerful men always play. Moving on my wife was completely different, however.

I ended up in the rocking chair in the doorway. I wanted the smell of Indian summer flowers, and the last September light of fireflies, and that smoky aroma that rolled down from the fir-lined slopes every fall.

What I wanted most of all was my wife.

If I'd had any sense of where she might have gone, I would've ridden there and tried to find her.

But I didn't. I can deal with just about anything except the feeling of helplessness. We were pretty much a pair. No close friends; no real social life; nobody we turned to — except each other — to confide in. There was no place to go.

Around seven, weary mentally and physically, I surprised myself by drifting into an uneasy sleep on top of the bed, Conner right next to me. He'd started making deep whining noises halfway up his windpipe. As if he knew what was going on and missed her, too. He laid his head on my bed. He smelled of heat and dog.

Something startled me awake.

In a single motion, I rolled over, yanking my six-gun free and pointing it at the open doorway.

"Gol, Marshal, don't shoot." Win Evans came inside. "She said you'd probably be here."

"Who did?"

"Why, Callie. Your wife."

"Oh." I rolled over so that I was sitting up. I rubbed my face and fired up the last of the hand-rolled cigarettes I'd been smoking when I went to sleep. "Where is she?"

"The town park."

"How'd she look?"

He shrugged, his eyes evasive. "Guess I didn't get a good look at her."

I stood up. "C'mon, Win. Don't bullshit me. How'd she look?"

"Scared."

"She say why?"

"No, she just asked me if I'd go get you

and tell you to come back to town."

"That's all she said?"

He nodded. "I s'pose I could've asked her some questions, Lane. But you're my boss and all. It wouldn't have been right."

"You did fine, Win. Just fine."

I was already pumping fresh water into the washbasin. I needed to start reviving myself.

"Anyhow, I wanted to get you the message."

"I appreciate it, Win," I said, toweling my face dry.

On the way back to town, he said, "I was wondering if this had anything to do with the trial tomorrow."

"That's what I was wondering, too."

He shrugged. "I guess you'll find out soon enough."

"Yeah, I guess I will."

When we reached town, he said, "I got to get back to my rounds, Lane. I'll see you later."

She wasn't at the park.

I walked every inch of it and couldn't find her. I sat down on a bench and rolled a cigarette and tried to make sense of it all. We both got letters that day, special letters packed with material Webley's Pinkertons had given him. She promised she'd explain everything tonight. But when I got there she wasn't home. And now she'd had me summoned to the park and she was nowhere to be found.

The Indian summer night was sweet with birdsong and river rush and the gleam of snow-peaked mountains in the moonlight. Far too precious a night to waste on the griefs of human beings, including my own.

But griefs I had, and the worst kind. I wasn't even sure what they were all about.

People strolled by on the boardwalk. The ones who recognized me waved and I waved back. I was glad they didn't come over to talk. Saloon music. Saloon laughter. Crack of billiard balls from down the street.

I was on my third cigarette when I saw her peek out of the alley down the block. Even from here, the furtive way she moved told me she was in trouble.

I ground out my smoke with the heel of my boot and waved to her. She waved in return, then vanished back into the shadow of the alley.

I was down there in moments. She came into my arms more desperately than she ever had before. We didn't say anything at first, just held each other. Her body was damp from exertion in the heat. Her breasts felt wonderful pushing against me. I traced the elegant bones of her face with my long fingers.

I led her down the alley to a small loading dock. There was a buckboard used for delivery sitting there. I lifted her up so she could sit on the edge of its bed.

"I got a letter, too," I said.

"I thought you would." Then: "You know why he did it, of course."

"Sure."

"He wants you to drop the charges against Trent."

"And that's what I'm going to do."

"What? Oh, no, Lane. No, you're not."

"I thought you liked it here. I thought you wanted me to drop charges."

"But not this way. Not now that he's resorted to something like this."

Neither of us spoke for a while. Then she said: "Somebody's following me, I think."

"You sure?"

"The man — the man the letter told you about — the man I was married to — he left a note for me at school. He wanted me to meet him tonight. That's where I've been."

"You think he's a part of it, Callie?"

"Of course. The Pinkertons were looking into my background. They turned David up. And he's been cooperating with them."

"Meaning that when all this gets out about you, he'll be here to confirm it."

"Exactly," she said. "Just the way Webley wants him to." Then: "I probably shouldn't have gone to his room. I'm sorry if that bothers you. Nothing — happened. I just asked him to leave town. We were married once — it was a terrible marriage and I was awfully young and naïve — but he doesn't care about that. He's still bitter that I divorced him. And he's still working all his confidence games and doing a lot of riverboat gambling. He'll never amount to anything. He'll be on Webley's payroll for a while and then when Webley's through with him, he'll find some other crooked way of making a living."

Visiting a man's hotel room. A former husband yet. Usually the jealousy I tried to control would have risen up and taken me over. All sorts of troubling images would have filled my mind. Images that would have been difficult to get rid of.

But not in this circumstance. It was pretty clear she hated him. He had the power to destroy her, and that seemed to

62

be exactly what he had in mind.

"You said you thought somebody was following you?"

She nodded. "I got that sense when I went to his room. I didn't see anybody, but somehow I knew he was behind me. I don't think I'm making it up. In fact — he may be watching us right now."

Ghost stories when you're a kid. Campfire nights. The boogeyman out there somewhere lurking in the unforgiving dark. I had that kind of moment now. My forearms were rough with gooseflesh. I touched my Colt for reassurance. I wasn't a kid anymore, and boogeymen now came in the shape of rich men who wanted you to do their bidding.

"Why don't we get out of here?" I said.

She nodded.

This time when I grabbed her waist, lifting her down from the bed of the buckboard, my fingers went higher. This time, on her right side, they contacted something wet. And, in the moonlight, dark. And for the first time I noticed that the front of her shirtwaist blouse was spattered with dark spots that glistened.

I thought of what she said about somebody following her.

As much as I wanted to ask her about

the dark spots on her dress, I suddenly wanted out of this alley.

I grabbed her hand and we started moving quickly toward the head of the alley.

All I could think of was those dark stains on her dress — stains that grew even more ominous in the lamplight — stains that I instinctively didn't want anybody else to see.

"Where're we going?" she said.

"The livery. I'll get us a wagon to take home."

"Are you all right?"

"People keep asking me that," I said, and there were many things in my voice at that second — anger, fear, dread — "and to be honest, no, no, I'm not all right. I'm not all right at all."

She started to say something and stopped. I didn't feel like talking either, had no idea what to say. Just wanted to walk, hard, fast, walk to the end of the world if I needed to.

And then someone was shouting my name. And I turned around and Tom Ryan was running after us, shouting, "There's trouble, Lane! There's trouble!"

SIX

This was unlike Ryan, shouting marshal business so that others in the street could hear him. He was usually discreet to the point of secrecy. Something must have shaken him. This was a night for surprises.

As he approached, his boots slamming against the wood of the boardwalk, I angled myself in front of Callie so that he could not see the heavy stains on the right side of her dress. "Don't move," I whispered. "I don't want him to see those stains."

She seemed about to explain, or maybe object, when he drew up to us. He took a moment to gather himself, taking several deep breaths, before he said, "They just came and told me."

"I'm afraid you lost me, Tom."

He shook his head in self-recrimination. He gulped a big breath of air, expelled it, touched his chest, and said, "At the church. Marie and I were helping build a few new pews when somebody from the hotel came over and told me about the dead man. I was on my way there now. Thought maybe you wanted to go along." He took another deep breath and said, "Evening, Callie."

"Evening, Tom." Was she suddenly pale or was it my imagination?

Back to me. "Figured if it's foul play, Lane, you ought to be there. You'll be in charge of it anyway. You and the doctor."

One of the things I changed immediately when I took over the town marshal's office was the sloppy way homicides were handled in this county. Doctors were brought in to give a medical opinion only at the end of the process. I made sure they were on the actual scene itself. I also made sure that they gave precise, written, articulate opinions as to how a person actually died. Homicides can be damned tricky. You think a man was clubbed to death, then you find out he'd actually had a stroke. These things make a big difference when you're charging somebody with a degree of murder and preparing to take him to trial.

I looked at Callie. "You want to just go on home, honey?"

It was important that Tom think that everything was all right between Callie and me. I was thinking ahead without realizing I was thinking ahead.

"Sure. I'll get supper on for us." She stood on tiptoes and kissed me on the cheek. I made sure Tom didn't get a chance to see her stains. And I turned her back around immediately, in the direction of the livery.

"See you in a while," I said.

Tom and I walked to the Excelsior Hotel. There was already a small crowd out front. Doesn't take long for word to spread. And murder is cheap entertainment. County fairs charge an admittance fee and you have to get yourself all spruced up. Murder is free and nobody cares how you look.

The interior of the Excelsior, the town's second-nicest hotel, was likewise packed. There's a taproom on the first floor and it had pretty much emptied into the lobby.

Mike Bryant, the burly owner and manager of the Excelsior, stood on the steps to the second floor, a Sharps cradled in his arms. "I locked the exit door from the outside, Lane. And I'm not letting anybody up or down."

"Appreciate it, Mike."

"You can bet your ass Morrissey's having himself a couple of good laughs on me tonight."

Morrissey ran The Chandler Arms, the

first-nicest place in Skylar. The men loathed each other. Bryant had a point. Murder was rarely good for hotel business.

Bryant let us pass. "Room fourteen, Lane."

There were four doors on each side of the second-floor hallway. All but one of them were open.

"When the hell can we go get some supper?" a drummer in suspenders and white shirt and checkered pants said from Room 10.

"Sorry about the inconvenience," I said. "But Mike did the right thing holding you folks here. My deputy Tom here'll be back to ask some questions."

The other rooms also held complainers. I'd probably be a little irritated if I had to sit and wait out the law, too. Especially if I was innocent.

He looked, this man named David Stanton, like the wax figure of a prominent stage actor. He was, or had been, a tall, somewhat fleshy man with dramatic good looks and a taste for the kind of expensive clothes — the dark suit, ruffled shirt, string tie, gold brocaded vest — that I always associate with large casinos and theaters. His face was frozen in an expression of surprise rather than fear, indicating that whoever had stabbed him — and the area around his heart was soaking wet with blood that had also soaked his right side and his lap — had done so quickly and with no warning. I thought of the blood staining Callie's dress, the spatters of it on her sleeves.

There was no murder weapon in sight. Tom began a thorough examination of the room, as did I. I'd taken him along to the last seminar I'd attended. The speakers spent a good deal of time discussing the methods used by British and French detectives working what they called "the crime scene." Previously, peace officers had spent only a brief amount of time going over the place where the victim was found. The French got down on their hands and knees with small rakelike objects, going over every inch of what they'd designated "the scene."

Tom took the west side of the room, I took the east. And thank God, too. That's where I found the button I recognized immediately. The button from the sleeve of Callie's shirtwaist blouse. I recognized it because I'd bought her that blouse with its triangular-shaped buttons for her last birthday.

I hesitated before stooping down and

picking it up. What if Tom saw me? And what if he then saw me pocket it?

But what choice did I have?

I glanced over my shoulder, stooped, picked it up, pocketed it.

Thankfully, Tom was searching the closet while I did all this.

Dick Zane from the undertaker's came then; and then Dr. Calendar, whom I used for most of the homicides; and then a youngster from the newspaper. He had a cigarette in his mouth and a derby on his head. The smoke from his cigarette kept twisting upward to his eyes and making him tear up. It kind of spoiled the hard-boiled impression he was hoping to make.

I held them all at bay in the hallway. It took us a good half hour to go over the room. Everybody was impatient. I didn't care. I wanted to do my job.

Every once in a while, I'd look at Stanton. I hated him and feared him and was jealous of him. He'd tried to destroy Callie in life but had failed; maybe he'd succeed in destroying her in death. I thought of how innocent and yielding she would have been back then; and of how cynically he'd taken her. That was the jealousy part, I guess. The hatred was for the way he'd made her part of his con games.

And the fear was for what he'd dragged her into through Webley.

The one thing I didn't find was money. Stanton should have had a lot of it, given his friendship with Webley. But he had only a few coins.

I spent the next hour talking with the guests on the second floor. I took half, Tom took half. They were cooperative but, if they were telling the truth, they were no help at all.

They hadn't heard an argument. They hadn't heard a scuffle. They hadn't seen Stanton enter or leave his room. They hadn't heard him call out for help. Most of them had been in their rooms.

I went downstairs to the staff.

The man on the night desk said that Stanton hadn't had any announced visitors. He said it was always possible that some-body had come in through the back door or even the fire escape. He brought the bellman over. He hadn't seen or heard anything, either. He had been on the second floor only once, though. The last time he'd talked to Stanton was around four o'clock. Stanton was in his room, having a drink of what appeared to be bourbon. He'd asked the bellman for two fresh towels.

The man behind the bar in the taproom

hadn't come on until six o'clock. He worked a seven-hour shift. He knew who Stanton was but hadn't seen him all evening. He had two customers who'd been sitting there since five o'clock or so. They hadn't seen Stanton either.

Back upstairs, the crowd had dispersed. They were getting ready to carry the body down on a stretcher. There was a blanket over Stanton now. Blood soaked through from his wound.

Tom was busy doing another sweep of the room. A couple of times I heard his knees crack when he bent down. He'd given up a good job with a local wheel manufacturer to become a deputy. His wife hadn't been all that happy about his decision, seeing it as a lark rather than a real job. He was forty, and a deputy's salary wasn't all that much when you could hear the arthritis cracking in your limbs when you got up and down. But he had a little boy's enthusiasm for his job, and I was glad he did.

"Anything?" I said when he was finished. He shook his head.

I hoped my sigh wasn't audible. If he'd found another button or anything like that —

"All right if we get him on the wagon now, Marshal?" Dick Zane said. We all like to think ill of undertaking people, but Dick was a family man, a helpful citizen who saw to it that the poor always got fed at Christmastime and whose wife did volunteer work in the hospital. "He's starting to smell."

I nodded approval. The body was taken away.

Mike Bryant, the hotel owner, came into the room. He looked pretty damned unhappy and I didn't blame him. "Three guests have already left. Afraid to stay here."

"I'm sorry, Mike. I really am. We're working as fast as we can."

"You get anything yet?"

"Not yet."

He shook his large head. "He looked like the kind."

"What kind you talking about?"

"Oh, hell, you know. Too slick by half. A ladies' man. He took several of the local boys for a lot of money last night at poker. They weren't happy about that. Especially when one of them started hinting he might have been cheating. But that's what they always say when they lose. Then there was Ken Adams."

"What about him?"

"Sometime yesterday, Stanton managed to meet Sylvia Adams, and sneaked her into his room last night."

"And Ken found out?"

"You bet he found out. He had a big scene with Sylvia and Stanton in the room here. I promised I wouldn't say anything to anybody about it. You know, to protect her reputation and all."

"Ken threatened Stanton?"

"He more than threatened him, Lane. He pulled a gun on him. That's when Sylvia came running downstairs and got me. I went up there with a sawed-off and got Ken calmed down. I felt sorry for him. Hell, he's just a kid. Even with a gun in his hand he looked pretty pathetic standing next to Stanton. Stanton didn't even look scared. He'd probably been through this kind of thing a hundred times before. With jealous husbands, I mean."

"So Ken put the gun away?"

"Ken put the gun away and Sylvia took him home. It was one of those things I wish I hadn't seen. I got a wife, too, Lane. If she ever did anything like that to me —" He shook his head. "Poor old Ken."

"I'll need to talk to him."

"I figured you would. That's why I told you. Maybe I should've told you this morning, huh?"

I shrugged. "No way of knowing it

would turn into something like this. And anyway, we don't know that Ken had anything to do with this."

"I sure hope not. He's a good lad."

"Yes, he is."

"And Sylvia seems like a good woman, as far as that goes."

I smiled. "She interviewed me as her ninth-grade school assignment when I first came here."

"Yeah, then she left school and married Ken. He wasn't but seventeen." He frowned. "I just hope he didn't have anything to do with this."

Behind me, Tom said, "Somebody might have seen him."

"Seen Ken?" I said.

Tom nodded. "Man down the hall — a drummer — said he saw somebody fitting Ken's description here earlier in the afternoon. Maybe about four."

Bryant said, "But Stanton wasn't killed till later."

"Anybody else see this man?" I said.

Tom shook his head. "But there's always the possibility Ken got here at a time when most guests were gone and hid somewhere."

"Such as?" Bryant said.

"No offense, Mr. Bryant, but it wouldn't

take a lot to pick the locks on one of your doors. What if he got inside Stanton's room and hid in the closet? Stanton comes in and they argue and Ken stabs him?"

"That's possible, I suppose," Bryant said. He glanced around the room. "A big fucking mess is what this is." He nodded to the door. "I better get back downstairs and see if anybody else has left because they're afraid to stay here." He frowned. "The Chandler Arms is gonna be full up tonight — with guests who left *my* place."

After he'd gone, Tom said, "Sounds like we've got at least one good suspect."

"Maybe. But I'm like Bryant. I sure hope Ken didn't do this. He's a good young man. Somebody like Stanton comes to town —"

I was doing what Bryant had been doing. I was putting myself in Ken Adams's place. Imagining what it would be like to walk in on your wife and another man in a hotel room — all that terrible rush of terror and rage and impotence — in a moment like that —

But maybe that was Ken Adams's best argument.

In the moment of fury itself, you might do something crazy. But after eighteen, twenty hours had passed? There was a good chance that you'd brought some per-spective to the situation. You'd still be angry, of course — hell, maybe you'd even told your wife to get out — but you'd be in much better control of your impulses. It was at least an even chance that you would have ruled out violence.

"We'll have to sort through all this," I said to Tom. "I don't want to accuse any-body of anything yet."

Least of all my wife, I thought.

"I agree," Tom said. "That's why I only mentioned it to you and Bryant." He sounded defensive.

"Good man."

He relaxed. He can work his jaw pretty hard when he's upset. "I probably shouldn't have said that, should I?"

"If that's the worst thing you ever do, Tom, you'll have led a perfect life. You should hear about some of the things I've said I shouldn't have."

I went back to the office. I'd learned at my last peace officer seminar to start a file on every major crime. List the name of the victim, the circumstances, the weapon, the names of the people interviewed, names that I'd written on a small tablet, as had Tom. I two-finger-typed all this on four sheets of paper, slapped a label reading

DAVID STANTON on it, and then set it on my desk.

I then wrote out a telegram to the Chicago police department asking for any information on David Stanton under that name or various aliases. I wrote a similar telegram to the Royalton Hotel. I'd have to wait till morning to send these.

I was still at my desk when the door opened and Trent Webley came in. "Evening, Marshal." He seemed quiet, sober.

"Evening, Trent."

"My dad's still over in his office. He's wondering if you'd stop over and see him."

"He could always stop over here."

He shrugged. "He's got a lot of work to do."

"So do I, Trent."

I didn't like the idea of being summoned. But then I decided I was being pissy for no particularly good reason. His office was two blocks away. I was still sound enough of limb to survive a trek as long as that.

I stood up. Grabbed my hat.

At this end of Center Street you wouldn't have known there'd been a murder. This was the section where the bank and the pharmacy and the general store and the other Main Street businesses were located. The windows were dark, the hitching posts empty, the lamplight properly sedate.

Trent had a key to let him into the bank. We went up a flight of stairs that ran adjacent to the bank on the first floor. The second-floor hallway was dark except for the yellow outline of a door at the far end. I could hear typewriter keys being punched at about the same rate I was capable of. While most typewriter users were female secretaries, the executive class couldn't help but try their luck, too. At about ten words a minute.

He had one of those inner sanctums. There was an outer office and a larger inner office and in the center of that office yet another office, like Chinese boxes. It was in this that Paul sat, pecking away at a Royal.

His office had the air of a judge's chamber, walnut wainscoting, a vast Persian rug, heavy dark furnishing, glassed-in bookcases filled with tomes that portended great and eternal knowledge.

He typed for a few more minutes to show me who was in charge, then turned in his tall executive chair, lifted a lighted cigar from an ashtray, and said, "Sit down and have one of my Cubans."

"No, thanks. I need to get back. It's a busy night."

"So I've been told."

"Your friend Stanton got himself murdered. But I'm sure you already know about that."

He smirked. "He was hardly my friend, Marshal. He just did me a few favors."

"Why did you want to see me, Paul?"

"To tell you that it isn't too late."

"Isn't too late for what?"

"For telling the county attorney that you've decided to drop the charges against Trent."

"I'm afraid I can't do that."

But I didn't sound as determined as I had earlier today. And he obviously heard a hint of wavering in my voice.

He leaned forward on his elbows. "This is distasteful to me, Marshal. You probably don't believe that. You probably think I enjoy pushing people around. And sometimes I do. I admit that. But not you. You've refused to go on my informal payroll, but you've given me plenty of room and I appreciate that. But as I said, I have my son to consider and my family name."

"What's this all mean, Paul, in plain English?"

"In plain English, Marshal, it means that your wife was in Stanton's hotel room tonight. I can produce two witnesses who saw her there. And when she left, she appeared to have blood on her clothes."

"I see."

"Maybe you don't see, Marshal," he said in his quiet way. "She was in his room. And I've got all kinds of information that establishes she was not only married to him once, but did everything she could to get away from him. She hated him."

He looked again at Trent, then back at me.

"How do you think all this would sound if the county attorney presented it to a grand jury, Marshal? You think it just might get your wife indicted for murder?"

SEVEN

Ken Adams had homesteaded land just to the east of town. He was one of those completely independent men who ask no help from anyone else but his wife. He and Sylvia built their own log cabin, dug their own well, and planted their own crops. I don't think he had a sinister past, but he lived as though he did. You saw him at church sometimes, and at the occasional social evening, but generally the Adamses and their children stayed to themselves. Sylvia was a dark-haired beauty whose hard work hadn't cost her a whit in femininity.

The only thing I knew about them was that she'd left him briefly on two or three occasions. I'd heard a lot of explanations for this — everything from her taking up with another man to her heading back to North Platte, Nebraska, her home, to tend to an ailing father — but gossip is rarely reliable, so I didn't have any real sense of their relationship. One time they came to town and Ken had a black eye. If Sylvia had had the black eye, that would have set the gossips to speculating overtime, ominously. But with Ken's eye being discolored, all that was made of it were a few stupid jokes.

As I drew my horse into the glade that opened on their small farm, I saw lights in the windows and heard a lonesome fiddle being played. The outbuildings were traced in the gold of moonlight. I ground-tied my horse and approached the house.

I was a hundred feet away when the door opened abruptly and a figure stood there silhouetted, moonlight glinting off the barrel of a rifle.

"You go back to town, Marshal. I did a very foolish thing tonight. And I'm sorry I did it, but I don't want to talk about it."

Even in silhouette, Sylvia's figure was pleasing to see.

"Is Ken in there?"

"He is but he doesn't want to talk to you either. Now, you scat." She waggled the rifle in my direction.

Full moon. Wind soughing through the bright, autumn-baked leaves. The scent of forest loam and clear stream water.

"I'll just come back with my deputies, Sylvia. You don't want it to get out of hand, do you?"

"It's already out of hand. I broke my

marriage vow." She hesitated. "Again. And now people'll blame poor Ken."

I wasn't sure what she was talking about. Blame poor Ken for what? Killing David Stanton?

"I'm going to come inside, Sylvia. Shoot me if you want to. But I'm not taking my gun out, and I'm not going back to town."

"The mood I'm in, Marshal, I just might do it."

"I don't think you will. You're too good a woman."

"Oh, I'm some good woman, all right. The things I've done to that poor husband of mine." She sounded about to cry; she also sounded frenzied, even a little crazy. Whatever she'd done, she'd paid a price for it in guilt.

I started walking.

She aimed the gun at my chest. "You heard me, Marshal."

I kept walking.

"Right now, I could do just about anything."

I was just about to the front stoop of the cabin before I realized that I hadn't heard any other voices from inside. Neither Ken nor the kids. They were awful quiet.

She didn't shoot me. What she did, when I was a few feet away, was retreat into the cabin. And lock it.

I hadn't worried about being shot. But I was worried about getting inside. Something was very wrong here.

I knocked on the door. "You need to let me in."

"I already told you, Marshal. Go away."

"Where are Ken and the kids?"

"He took them to the Chandlers. He's going to stay there tonight."

"He shouldn't have left you alone."

"I told him to."

"We all make mistakes, Sylvia. You and Ken need to sit down and talk about this."

"I warned him. Before we were married, I mean, I warned him how I was. How I sometimes — I just went off with other men. How I just can't seem to help myself. The other two times — at least it was out of town where I didn't embarrass him. But this time — right in Skylar. Right where everybody can find out. Just think of what my little ones are going to hear at school. All the things they'll have to hear about their mother."

"Why don't you let me in?"

"I don't want to see you. I don't want to see anybody. Not ever again."

"Sylvia, listen, please —"

There was just the one shot and it was

oddly muffled, and it was followed by a tiny squeaky sound, almost like the mewling of a newborn kitten, and then there was just that awful silence that follows death. My horse whinnied for no good reason — that was the first sound to break the silence. And then the night birds in the forest began to sing in a way that was almost like crying.

I didn't bang on the door, I didn't call out, I didn't run to my horse and head back to town for help. There was no sense to any of that.

I was narrow enough to shinny myself sidewise through a northern-pointing window. She was slumped over in a rocking chair. The six-shooter hung from two of her fingers, angled down across her bosom. She'd put the barrel to her temple. Not even death could destroy the small, perfect, almost doll-like features of her face. The eyes looked stunned and sad at the same time.

I went and unbolted the door, and went out and got on my horse and rode over to the Chandler farm. I was thinking about everything and nothing. It was one of those moments when your mind keeps flitting around, unable to light on any one subject for long. There were so many things to think about. If Sylvia had killed Stanton, then Callie was not in any trouble. But I couldn't be sure of that. She'd certainly been remorseful. But that could have just been about sleeping with Stanton.

The Chandler farm was pretty much like the Adams farm. They were homesteaders, too, though not anywhere as self-reliant. Verne Chandler, who wasn't yet thirty, had had a bad stroke his first year here in Skylar, and people still had to pitch in from time to time to help him support himself. Fortunately for him, Am Chandler is a purposeful, smart, and resourceful woman who can do damned near any job a man can, and likely do it better. She's not much for charity, and always looks uncomfortable and a little embarrassed when neighboring farmers and ranchers stop by at certain points in the year. Verne is still paralyzed on the right side of his body. Things aren't likely to get better for him. They had but the one boy — I never knew why they didn't have more children — but he passed the last time smallpox made a sweep of our part of the state. Six, he'd been. Am Chandler had not had an easy life.

Verne came to the door, a fortyish man crabbed and bent before his time. He always wore a heavy sweater, even in the summertime. The stroke had somehow affected his thyroid and left him constantly cold. His bald head shone in the moonlight as he stuck his head outside. "Don't talk loud," he said. "Ma, she's just put the two kids down for the night." He spoke in a way that made some people think he was slow or tetched. He was neither. He'd just suffered a stroke.

"I need to talk to Ken."

"You want to come in?"

"Need to talk to him out here, Verne."

He nodded and dragged himself back inside. He'd been one hell of a Sunday afternoon baseball player. It was hard to watch him in his present state.

Ken Adams came out and said, "Something wrong, Marshal?"

"Let's walk down to the creek."

He shrugged and closed the door quietly behind him, and followed me out to where the grass was long and silver-tipped from the moon.

The one thing the seminars don't prepare you for is telling somebody that his wife is dead. Long as I'd been at this, I'd never figured out how to do it with any skill. Later on, I'd always think of ways I could have been gentler, kinder.

The creek smelled fresh in the night. An occasional fish slapped to the surface. Been a long time since I'd been on a camping trip, eating freshly caught fish from a pan set on a campfire. It sounded good now. Almost everything sounded good now — except saying what I had to say.

"Something wrong, Marshal?" he said again. Ken Adams was a slender, towheaded man with wiry strength and a somber, insular personality ideal for the frontier. The frontier demanded a certain stoicism from its survivors, and Ken Adams was stoic enough for any six men. Except — and understandably — when he caught his wife in another man's hotel room.

I rolled a cigarette as we walked. I said, thinking of no other way to do it, "I went to your place to see you and Sylvia. She killed herself, Ken."

And damned if he didn't haul out his Bull Durham and build himself a smoke and get it lighted before he said a word. The only sign that he'd heard me was in his dark eyes. They glistened with quick tears.

"How'd she do it?"

"A Colt."

"She leave a note?"

"Not that I could see."

"You were the one who found her?"

"I talked to her first. She bolted herself in the cabin. She wouldn't let me in."

He took a deep drag from his smoke and exhaled in a stream. The smoke was blue in the moon rays. "She say anything before she did it?"

"How sorry she was."

"Anything else?"

"That she was ashamed. And that she worried how the other kids would treat yours at school."

He said, and without any rancor, "She wasn't no whore."

"I don't think she was."

"And nobody better say she was. Not to my face anyway."

"I'm sorry, Ken."

"She warned me how she was. Sometimes she just — strayed. This was the only time she ever done it here, in town."

"She said that, too."

"That Stanton, he was workin' on her the first time he was here. And then the second time they got together."

Something about that wasn't right, what he'd just said. "You said 'the first time.' He was here more than once?"

"He was here about a month ago. He met her in the library. He was askin' her all kinds of questions about Paul."

A very different story from the one Webley had told me about hiring the Pinkertons.

"And she wasn't the only one Stanton shined up to either."

"Another woman, you mean?"

"He must've liked 'em married. I knew a fella down in Tulsa like that. He liked 'em married. Said they was more fun 'cause it was kinda dangerous and all. You know, the husband out there somewhere with a gun."

"You know who this other woman was?"

He shook his head. "They had a fight about her, I guess. Him and Sylvia. She went up to his room and heard some other woman there. They was arguin' about that when I got there."

I hesitated. "Did you kill him?"

"I sure wanted to."

"That's not an answer."

"I wanted to but I didn't."

"Did Sylvia kill him?"

He sobbed. He'd fought so hard against showing me anything — some misdirected sense of manliness, I guess — that it burst out and he couldn't stop it. A sob of the kind a woman would make. "She always said she never cared about them no other way except the thrill of it. I guess she was a little like that fella down in Tulsa I mentioned. But this Stanton — I guess she felt somethin' for him 'cause she got jealous when she found out about this other woman."

I said again, "Did she kill him, Ken?"

"I don't think so."

"You're not sure."

"She went down there again tonight."

"Did you?"

"Yeah. I followed her into town, if that's what you mean."

"You go to his room?"

He nodded.

"What happened?"

"He was dead," he said. "Maybe I would've killed him if somebody hadn't beat me to it."

EIGHT

Toomey and Grice were in my office when I got back to town.

"Well?" Toomey said.

"Well, what, Walter?"

"Well, did you arrest him?"

"And who would 'him' be?"

"Who would 'him' be?" Phil Grice said. "Ken Adams, of course."

I shook my head. I pitched my hat on top of the bookcase, sat down with my cup of coffee, and rolled myself a cigarette as I went through Sylvia's suicide and Ken's denial.

"And you believed him?" Grice said.

"Not necessarily. But I didn't — and don't — disbelieve him either."

"He had a damn good motive," Grice said.

"And people saw him in the room," Toomey said.

I smiled. "You want to get saddled up and all three of us'll ride out and lynch him?" They were the two most prominent businessmen on the town council. They were sleek and well-fed and as full of their own self-promoting bullshit as anybody in Skylar County. Toomey owned two stage lines and a short-haul railroad, and Grice oversaw his daddy's varied business interests, sort of the way Paul did, but less successfully. They both had eyes on seats in the state legislature.

"You're forgetting, Marshal, what happens the day after tomorrow." Grice gave Toomey a smug smile.

I was confused. Tomorrow was the trial. But what about the day after?

Toomey said, "The lieutenant governor is coming here. Phil and I convinced him to spend a day with us. And we certainly don't want some sordid murder hanging over our heads."

I'd forgotten about the lieutenant governor, whose name I couldn't remember anyway. "So you want me to just arrest somebody, is that it?"

"Well, it would look better if we had somebody charged with it and in jail," Toomey said. They were both too stout to wear the kind of sharply cut suits they did, but that didn't deter them, of course. They wore matching pearl-colored derbies, too.

"And you could always let him go free after the lieutenant governor left," Grice said.

I laughed. Couldn't help it. "I'm glad law and order means so much to you. Murder isn't much more than an inconvenience to you, is it?"

"Is it wrong to have civic pride?" Grice said.

"Some hayseed kills a visitor," Toomey said. "How does that look to important people, do you think?"

"A 'visitor'? You two know anything about David Stanton?"

"He came into the taproom several nights," Grice said. "He was a well-traveled man. He had a lot of wonderful stories."

"I'll bet he did. And I'll bet at least half of them were true, too."

"He was an educated man," Grice said. "He talked about how either Phil or I could become governor if we wanted to."

You couldn't go wrong buttering up two pampered blowhards like these two. Easy enough to imagine Stanton painting them pictures of themselves as great national leaders rising up to lead the masses to the promised land.

"You sure he didn't mention anything about the presidency?"

Grice said, "I'm going to ignore that, Marshal. You've obviously come to the conclusion that you should have arrested

Ken Adams. And now you're going to try to make yourself look better by belittling us."

Deke Newton, my senior night deputy, came in. "There's somebody up front who says he's got information about the murder. Says he saw something he wants to report. You want me to handle it or you want to?"

Toomey said, "I don't mean to be rude here, Deke, but when you've got two members of the town council talking to the high marshal, isn't it obvious that you should handle this yourself?"

Deke started to say something, and then stopped. What was the point of trying to be reasonable with two legendary national leaders like these?

"You handle it, Deke. I'll talk to you later."

Deke nodded and left.

"I'm sort of surprised he couldn't have figured that one out for himself," Grice said.

I usually saw these two only at town council meetings, the other two members of which acted as my protection. They kept Grice and Toomey from doing their pompous worst, and interrupted their orating whenever it looked as if I might jump up and do sizable damage to their sizable frames.

"Now," Grice said, "where were we?"

"I think you were asking me to arrest somebody before the lieutenant governor gets here so we can tell him that the murder is solved and the kingdom of Skylar is safe again."

"You don't have to take that tone with us," Toomey said.

This would have been something for all the schoolkids to overhear. There were too many towns where the law would give in to two showboats like these and jail a possibly innocent man just to make things look good.

"I do when you're asking me to do something this shoddy. I admit he's a strong suspect. And he admits he was in the room and had seriously thought of killing Stanton. But he said Stanton was dead when he got there. I have to weigh what he said against his wife committing suicide. There's at least as good a possibility that she killed Stanton. I wanted to give him at least a little while with his kids. Their lives have just come apart. They need their father. I'm looking to ride out there tomorrow noon and talk to him some more. If he looks any better for it, I'll arrest and bring him back here."

"Well," Grice said, "why didn't you say so?"

"I didn't say so" — keeping my temper in check — "because I didn't want to give you the impression that I was going along with your scheme to throw somebody in jail before the lieutenant governor gets here. What I'm doing tomorrow is what I would do under any circumstances, whether you'd come in here tonight or not."

They looked happy. Fat and sleek and happy. Despite what I'd just said, they were obviously convinced that they'd talked me into cooperating with them.

"You say noon?" Grice said.

"Yes," I said. "Noon. Why?"

"I was wondering if you couldn't make it earlier," Grice said.

"Can't. I have to be in court tomorrow morning. Trent Webley's trial."

Toomey glanced at Grice and then at me. "You mean you didn't hear?"

"Hear what?"

"About the trial tomorrow."

A deep and terrible sickness began to form somewhere in my stomach. "What about it?"

Toomey said, "It's been called off. The judge came down with a terrible case of the gout. Trial's been postponed at least a week."

"So you can go out to Adams' place bright and early tomorrow morning," Grice said.

They said some other things, too, but I didn't hear them, or if I did they didn't register. All I could think about was the judge and what Paul had used on him to get the trial called off.

I needed to get out of the office, get home, before I confronted Webley and made even more trouble for myself.

NINE

She was gone when I got home.

A lamp burned on the table. A meal of cold beef and a boiled potato and a slice of pumpkin pie had been set out for me. I had a drink instead.

I sat in the squeaky hardwood rocking chair my grandfather had brought with him from Kilarney and tried to sort through everything that had happened today and tonight.

All I knew for sure was that Paul had lied to me about hiring Pinkertons and I was pretty sure why. He'd wanted to impress me, intimidate me with his sweeping powers to counter anything I might do. And that way I'd give in to him. A seedy blackmailer coming to him was much less impressive.

David Stanton was dead. I had three suspects, two I was willing to talk about, Ken and Sylvia Adams. The third suspect was my wife.

I knew one other thing as well: I'd been bushwhacked. I hadn't thought of Paul getting to Judge Pickett. Pickett was a fusty old bastard, and we'd never been friends, but his rectitude was beyond question. But he was human, meaning that sometime, somewhere he'd committed an indiscretion that Paul had been able to find out about.

My world tonight was a very different one from my world this morning, when I'd been happy to play the role of the middle-aged lawman to a brood of schoolkids eager to hear dime-novel tales of derring-do.

I wondered if Callie had killed him.

I was still wondering this when she came in the door, carrying a wicker basket she used to carry things down to the creek for a sturdy washing. Most of our things she washed in the galvanized tub. But things that got stained badly needed a pounding and scraping against wet, coarse rock.

She set the basket down and said, "I couldn't get the blood out."

She sounded and looked weary. She came over to the table and sat down across from me. The bourbon bottle sat in front of her. She poured herself a drink in a glass she'd used earlier. I'd never seen her take a drink before.

She said, "I didn't kill him."

"Then what was the blood?"

"I — was trying to make sure he was

101

dead. I'm sure I was hysterical. He — he'd been my husband once. As much as I hated him, I still didn't want him dead."

"Be careful you don't make me cry."

She glared at me. "So you're going to be jealous? That's all you can think of at a time like this? To be jealous?"

All the jealousy I hadn't felt earlier tonight in the park when she'd given me a partial version of the truth — now it was upon me. I was at my cold worst. "How many times did you see him?"

She shrugged, looked away. "Four, I guess."

"You guess?"

"I didn't keep track. It wasn't anything I wanted to remember."

"Why'd you see him?"

"You're treating me like one of your suspects."

"You *are* one of my suspects."

"Oh, great, Lane. Just great."

"Answer my question."

"Quit talking to me that way." Then: "He said if I didn't see him he'd tell people about me — about us."

"But you didn't think to tell me?"

"Tell you that I was a wanted felon with a reward on my head?"

"I deserved the truth."

She stared at me. The anger faded in her blue eyes. "Yes, you did," she said softly.

"Sylvia Adams killed herself tonight."

"Oh, my God."

"She was seeing him, too."

The anger was back. "Oh, no, you don't, Lane. You don't make it sound like I was seeing him for the same reason she was. She was going to bed with him. I wasn't."

"He didn't try and get you in bed?"

"Of course he did. But I wouldn't go. All I was doing was trying to stall him, figure out how to handle him before he put the word out about me."

"That's why you were there tonight?"

"I was there tonight," she said, the anger still cold and hard in her voice, "because I wanted to see if he was the one who'd sent me that envelope."

"He wasn't."

"What?"

"Paul was."

"Webley —"

"Stanton tracked you down somehow. There weren't any Pinkertons. He went to Webley directly. He was in town twice."

"Twice? That I didn't know."

"Well, he sure knew about you. And he must've picked up that Webley was looking for some sort of weapon to use against me so I'd drop the charges against Trent."

"But you're not going to."

"That's sort of a moot point now." I told her about Judge Pickett.

"Oh, Lane, I'm sorry." Then: "Oh, my Lord, what a mess."

She came over and sat in my lap the way she did sometimes, and we rocked in the noisy chair. I listened to the night and watched the play of a shaft of moonlight on a boulder near the front of our land. There was so much to say and nothing to say. She was woman and child at this moment; and I felt like man and boy. Both of us were undone by it all.

And then we were in bed and conjoined as much in spirit as in body, solace as much as sex being what we were after, the gentility of it being exactly what I needed. I didn't doubt her then, not at all, and told her so and told her I was sorry for how I'd interrogated her. And then I remembered that Deke had brought a witness in, a witness I'd forgotten to check out myself.

But then she was holding me and we made love for the second time and I forgot all about Deke and the witness, forgot everything as we brought the covers up over us, the night suddenly chill, and cuddled like children, her falling asleep in my arms the way she used to long, long ago when we'd first been married.

I slept too, hard and deep and long, and when I woke up I heard ridiculously happy morning birds and saw a ridiculously beautiful slant of sunlight through our window. I then slipped in and out of sleep for a time, knowing I needed to get up but not wanting to, purposely keeping certain thoughts at bay for a time, just enjoying the texture of her sleep-warm skin and the distinct sweet scent of her hair.

And then it was all gone, ruined, smashed by a fist meeting our door several times, a knocking sound that bore no good.

My first word of the day — a word that would later seem appropriate to the entire day — was "Hell."

"I wonder who it is."

"Nobody I want to see, that's for sure."

I got up, snagging my Colt from the holster on the floor, dragging myself to the door in the butternuts I struggled into.

Tom Ryan stood there. He looked both sleepy and upset. His horse was ground-tied on the edge of our property.

"I'm sorry about this."

"What's wrong?"

"I thought I'd better warn you."

"Warn me about what?"

He told me in his usual manner. Carefully, thoroughly, and as objectively as possible. He waited till the end to make his personal comment. "I don't believe the sonofabitch, of course. But some people might."

It was a day for the fishing hole. Take a pipe and a good book along. Even if you didn't catch anything, the day would be its own reward, the lazy sunlight on the lazy river and all the forest creatures that came to the bank to give you a quick inspection. And then heading home just as the sunset was streaking that rose color particular to Indian summer dusks. A damned good day.

Unlike the day I was facing now.

"Where is he?"

"Deke let him go. Didn't have any reason to hold him."

I shook my head, trying to clear it. "I need to get to the office. I'll be there in half an hour or so. Put on some fresh coffee, will you?"

"Sure." He put his hand out and touched my shoulder. "I feel like shit telling you about this, Lane."

"Thanks."

I went back inside. Callie was already

up, making coffee. I went to the sink and pumped some water and started cleaning up. I gave myself a spit bath, shaved, put on clean clothes.

When I was sitting at the table tugging on my Texas boots, Callie said, "You going to tell me, or do I have to find out for myself?"

"A punk named Hastings," I said. And paused. I wasn't sure how to say the rest of it.

She came over and sat down across from me. "You going to finish that sentence about a punk named Hastings?"

"He's a gunny. Or thinks he is. Or wants to be. Just some punk drifter. Anyway, he's been reading too many dime novels. He thought I killed Sansom so he wanted to have a gunfight with me."

"A gunfight?" she said. "Nobody has gunfights anymore."

"Tell *him* that, not *me*. Anyway, I went up to his room and took the bullets out of our respective guns, and then challenged him to a fight without bullets."

"That old trick of yours still work?"

"Works fine. At least it did that morning. He saw that I could beat him, so he decided maybe a gunfight wasn't such a good idea. I told him to be on a train or coach by yesterday afternoon."

"He didn't go."

"Oh, he went all right. I had Bob Sanchez put him on the train personally. The thing is, he obviously came back."

"And made some kind of trouble?"

This was going to be the difficult part. Telling her what he'd been saying over the course of a long night in town following the murder of David Stanton.

"I have a feeling that Paul put him up to it."

She sat there in her blue cotton robe, pretty even in her mussed morning way. I could see in her eyes and the tension in the angle of her long white neck that she knew what was coming. She appeared to be holding her breath. And then she said, before I could say it, "He's been telling people about me, hasn't he? Me and David?"

"Yeah."

"So everybody knows."

"Those who don't will know sometime this morning."

"Wanted felon teaching schoolchildren."

"Maybe people will have more faith in you than that."

She smiled sadly and touched my hand. "You know better than that, Lane. I can just hear Grice and people like that now.

I'll sound like Mary Magdalen, before they're through with me. They'll never let me go inside that schoolhouse again. And I imagine the county attorney will press charges."

"We'll get a lawyer. A good one."

"We'll have to move."

I took her hand. "Honey, right now that's not the important thing. Not legally."

She studied me as if I'd just spoken in a foreign language she didn't understand. "Not legally? What're you saying?"

"I'm saying that if that's the only story Hastings was pushing, we could probably handle it. The worst that would happen is that you'd have to go back to Chicago and face charges. But there are enough mitigating circumstances — you didn't have anything to do with Stanton cheating that old widow out of her money, you just happened to be married to him is all — that a good lawyer can probably get you off without too much trouble. Especially since you've led such a good life since you left Chicago."

"Then what's the trouble?"

"That isn't all Hastings is saying."

She studied me some more. "What else?"

"He claims he followed you to the hotel

where Stanton was."

"Oh, Lord."

"And," I said, "he claims he heard you stab Stanton and then saw you run away."

TEN

Eyes.

I'd had to escort a man past his family once. I was taking him to prison where he would be hanged. His folks didn't yell at me or scream at me. They just watched me as if trying to take my measure, as if trying to understand me and how I could do the job I did.

Eyes.

I'd seen a man totally withdraw from reality one day when the riverboat he was on sank and he was unable to save his four-year-old son from drowning. The look in his eyes was unfathomable, and I doubt he ever recovered in any but the most superficial way.

Eyes.

I'd once arrested two white men who'd drunkenly kidnapped a young Indian man, skinned him, and then set him on fire. The town I was marshal of then was not exactly a hotbed of affection and esteem for Kiowa. But their act had been so savage, so unimaginable, that when I brought them into town the crowd, which later tried to lynch them, gaped at them as if they were a species from some other world.

Eyes.

They were on me this morning.

Various eyes held various expressions. The people who hated me — and no town marshal is without his enemies — smiled with their eyes. The people who respected me — and thankfully, there were far more of those — offered me looks of pity and concern. But most of the eyes were just curious.

Just about everybody in town, it seemed, had heard Hastings's story already, and it was barely seven o'clock.

His wife, the marshal's wife, she was married once to that Stanton fella. They were grifters. There's a warrant out for her. And this young gunny, this Hastings kid — and I ain't sayin' I got any truck with him, because I don't — this Hastings kid, he swears he followed Callie Morgan up to this Stanton's room and listened at the door while she murdered him. I wonder what the marshal's gonna do. You think he'll arrest his own wife? You think he should be marshal while somethin' like this is goin' on? He's always been so high-and-mighty about the law and all. Be interestin' to see how he handles this.

Nobody said this out loud, at least not to me. But they didn't need to say it out loud. Their eyes said it for them.

Grice wasn't waiting for me, but Toomey was. When I came in he was obviously giving Tom a speech about me because they both looked guilty when I came across the threshold.

"Morning, gentlemen," I said.

"Morning," Tom said, as if he hadn't already seen me.

"I hope you can spare a few minutes for me," Toomey said. He sported another flashy city suit. This one was tan and made his girth appear even larger. "We had a brief breakfast meeting — the town council and I — and I think you should know some of the things that were said there."

Tom looked uncomfortable. "I'm going upstairs and getting the prisoners ready for day court."

"Thanks, Tom," I said.

"Fine man," Toomey said when Tom was gone.

"Yes, he is."

"Your office is a much better place for our meeting than up here in front."

"You're probably right. Coffee?"

"I've had too much already. It's hell on my hemorrhoids."

We got settled in chairs, my office door closed. "This young Hastings fellow told the council quite a story." He hadn't been kidding about his hemorrhoids. He squirmed around a lot, and occasionally winced.

"I'll bet he did."

"For one thing, he said you tried to run him out of town because you knew he was going to tell the truth about your wife."

"I appreciate all the faith you have in me."

"You didn't try to run him out of town?"

"I sure did. But only because he wanted to draw me into a gunfight."

"He didn't mention that."

"I don't imagine he did."

He lit a large cigar. He looked like one of those robber barons in the political cartoons. He probably enjoyed looking that way. "Do you know what he said about your Callie?"

"If you mean was she once married to Stanton, yes. If you mean is there a felony warrant out for her arrest, yes, though she isn't guilty. If you mean did she go to his hotel room the night he was murdered, yes. If you mean did she kill him, no."

"You're positive of that?"

"Yes."

114

"I used the word 'positive,' Marshal. That's a strong word."

"So's Callie's word. I asked her straight out and she told me straight out. She said that she'd gone to his room, found him dead, tried to see if she could revive him, and then ran away, scared."

"And you believe her?"

"You're going to make me damned mad here in another minute. Of course I believe her."

"I'm not trying to rile you."

"Well, you're doing a good job of it even if you're not trying."

"If she didn't kill him, who did?"

"Last night," I said, "you were sure of Ken Adams."

He frowned. "I guess you were right not to be."

"Thanks for admitting it."

"We're just worried about the impression we make on the lieutenant governor."

"I'm aware of that." I assumed by "we" he meant more himself and Grice than the town itself.

He took a long drag on his cigar, removed the cigar from his mouth, and studied it a moment. "We had a vote. Two to two."

"Two of you — that would be you and Grice — voted that I should step down until we know to your satisfaction that Callie didn't murder Stanton. And the other two voted to let me stay on for a while."

"You must have a crystal ball."

"Don't need it. Not where the town council is concerned."

"It's nothing personal."

"No, of course not."

"As I said last night, I really don't like it when you take that tone."

"So what's the decision? Do I take off my badge and hand it over?"

He shook his head. "You know how Rollie Limbaugh likes to compromise. He voted to give you twenty-four hours more and we went along with it."

"Reluctantly."

"Of course reluctantly, Marshal. How do you think this looks to the town? Here you're supposed to be investigating a murder and your wife is a suspect? If the lieutenant governor hears about this, he'll never —"

"— help you run for the state house?"

He flushed bourbon red. "You don't think I love this town?"

"This may surprise you, Toomey. But I'm sure you do love this town. But I'd bet you love yourself just a bit more."

He glowered. "As far as I'm concerned, you can hand in your badge right now."

"I'm going to surprise you again, Toomey, and agree with you."

"Are you serious?"

I took off my badge and tossed it on the desk in front of him. "Tom should be the one doing the investigating now. No matter how good a job I'll do, everybody's going to question my motive and my honesty."

He stared at the silver badge in front of him. "I don't believe you just did that."

I smiled coldly. "I almost don't believe it either."

ELEVEN

A few minutes after Toomey left, my badge in his pocket, Tom Ryan came back and said, "What the hell are you doing, Lane?"

"It's already done."

"None of us here wants you to quit."

"I didn't know I had to check with you on my personal matters."

"You sure as hell do if it involves you leaving."

I stood up. "I guess I'll go see how my money's doing."

He usually grinned when I brought up the subject of my investment, and made some kind of reference to me as a tycoon. But not today. "So what the hell am I supposed to do?"

"Just what Toomey and Grice want you to do, Tom. Become town marshal. And arrest somebody for Stanton's murder before the lieutenant governor gets here tomorrow."

"That's crazy talk."

"No, that's Grice talk. And Toomey talk."

"It really does piss me off, Lane. You're

putting me in a hell of a bind."

"What bind?"

He shook his head as if talking to a dense child. "What bind? Choosing between you and the town council. By rights, I should walk out with you."

"No, you shouldn't."

"You brought me on. You taught me. Whatever I know about bein' a peace officer, I learned from you."

"Then take what you learned and be a good town marshal. You're the obvious choice. And I know you can use the extra money."

But that wasn't all that was on his mind, and he knew I knew it. "And as for questioning Callie, that's part of the job, too," I said.

"She's your wife."

"She's my wife, and you're the town marshal. If she was your wife, I'd question her in a minute."

"She didn't do it."

"You don't know that for a fact. I know she didn't do it because I love her and trust her and take her word for things. But you're a lawman. She used to be married to Stanton. She was afraid of him and she hated him. And she was in his room the night of the murder. You have to question her."

"And you're gonna let me?"

"How am I going to stop you, Tom? You're wearing the badge now."

He sighed, shook his head again. "This is so damned strange, Lane. It just happened so — fast. It doesn't make any sense. You're the town marshal here — or should be."

I gave him the best smile I could muster. "I want to go check on my millions now."

Back in the late 1860s, it was assumed that Denver would get the transcontinental railroad. But then the Union Pacific elected to run track on the northern route through Cheyenne, arguing that the Denver route was too mountainous. Denver retaliated a few years later by building the Denver Pacific line that connected to the Union Pacific. Several small towns around Skylar raised some Eastern capital and voted to make Skylar the terminal for a similar line linking us to the Union Pacific, too. I'd saved some money over the years and invested it in this narrow-gauge line being built.

There was a hill on the eastern edge of town where you could sit your horse and watch the rail crews laying track. From here there was a beauty, even a poetry, to the hard and relentless work of the crews.

It's always easy to find beauty in somebody else's labor. You're not doing the sweating and the hurting. You don't have the crew bosses on your tail twelve hours a day.

But whenever I needed to comfort myself — the way my solitary old tomcat used to comfort himself by licking his massive paws — I took to the hill and spent an hour or so watching the gleaming silver tracks take sparkling shape in the sunlight. There were plenty of good reasons to hate the railroads, namely how they'd disrupted the lives of Indians and whites alike. But when you considered the mountains they'd blasted through, the bitter winters and scorching summers their workers had endured to build them, and the prosperity they brought to some of the poorer agricultural areas, you had to be in awe of their plain cussed competence, if not their indifference to the lives of the men who were laying the track.

I didn't have any big dreams myself. Just dreams of a cabin back in the Midwest where I'd been raised. I was one of those strange birds who actually enjoyed winter, so I actually suggested that a few times to Callie. Since she didn't share my fondness for the cold months, I needed to do a lot more persuading before I'd find myself among the Swedes up north. But the railroad would give us a nice retirement. The farmers in our county needed a closer shipping point for their crops. Skylar was central to several communities and would be ideal. The investment sure seemed like a good one.

I didn't stay quite the full hour as I usually did. I was able to spend the first twenty minutes or so lost in the spectacle below. But gradually I realized I couldn't keep the events of the last twenty-four hours away any longer. I started thinking about Stanton and who might have killed him. It would be easier for everyone but her two kids if we could prove that Sylvia Adams killed him. Easier for me and my wife anyway. I wasn't thinking as a lawman. I was thinking as a husband.

I was just turning my horse back toward town when I saw the tall, elderly man riding toward me. For someone his age and his health — he'd fought the cancer sometime back and had survived it — he rode with surprising ease and poise. I'd always thought that Edgar Bayard was the man Paul wanted to be, the kind of man who just quietly becomes the leader of any group he becomes a part of simply because he inspires trust.

His virtue isn't a handsome face. If anything, he's ugly, the pocked skin of youth
stretched tight over his jagged, gaunt features. The nose is a weapon, the mouth a
thin line, the jaw shovel-shaped. But something in the somber eyes and the wise, res-
onant voice holds you. You listen and are
impressed with what you hear.

"I hope we're both making a little money
today, Marshal," he said, nodding to the
tableau below in the valley.

"I'm making so much I decided to re-
tire."

"So I heard. That's why I rode out here,
in fact."

He wore a white shirt, dark riding
trousers, knee-length cordovan leather
boots. His horse was midnight black. His
white hair was long as a mountain man's
and the muscles in his narrow hands
corded and fierce. He'd survived the Indian wars and the Civil War with admi-
rable facility. He carried neither gun nor
knife. The last time he was attacked by a
man with a gun — this happened when he
was a customer in a bank one day and two
holdup men came in — he was shot in the
shoulder but managed to stomp one of the
robbers so badly that the man was crippled
for life. The other one he choked to death.

He'd been in his late sixties then.

"You did just what Paul wanted you to."

"I expect I did."

"I'm being selfish, Lane. I don't want my grandkids to grow up in a town that belongs to Paul."

"It belongs to him now."

"Not all of it. You didn't. Two members of the town council don't. I want to get this Stanton thing cleared up and pin that badge back on you."

Edgar Bayard had been a partner of Paul's for many years. They'd run silver mines together and had prospered. One of the mines was located on land belonging to the Ute Indians. It was widely known that Webley had initially wanted to start a fight with the Utes so that he would have a pretext to seize the land with the help of the Army. But Bayard had made the deal with the Utes, promising to give them a decent percentage of the mine's profits, and he didn't want to betray that trust. He had no special liking for Indians. But he did have a liking for his reputation. His word was his word. It took Paul seven years to achieve what he wanted. During the long year when the cancer took Bayard — and when most folks assumed he would soon die — Paul brought in some

Pinkertons who forced some Indians into a gun battle, reporting it to the local Indian agent as an attack. Webley had one of the state senators appeal to the Bureau of Indian Affairs, and he was permitted to break his deal with the Utes. Bayard wasn't strong enough physically to fight him. But when he heard what Webley had done, he insisted on being bought out. The two men had not spoken since.

"Maybe it's time for me to move on, Edgar."

"I meant what I said about my grandkids."

"You've got your own reasons for going up against Webley, Edgar."

"You should, too, Lane. He's been after you since the day you were sworn in."

"There's a Paul in every town, Edgar. When you've been a lawman as long as I've been, you get used to them."

He fixed me with those Old Testament eyes of his and said, "I'm following up a rumor I heard. Don't make any other decision until you hear from me."

"I don't even get a hint?"

"No."

"I assume it involves Paul."

The eyes were bitter now. His usual poise was gone for the moment. He was just one more pissed-off human being like the rest of us. He still had that fine speaker's voice, though. "He's got it coming, Lane. And maybe this time he's going to get it."

"Some people think my wife may have killed Stanton."

"You know Callie better than that and so do I. She's one of the finest women in this valley. She did something foolish when she was young. She took up with a scoundrel. But we've all done foolish things. You grow past them."

I smiled. "Hard to imagine you doing foolish things, Edgar."

He snorted. "Every night I lie in bed and think of all the stupid things I've done and said in my life. And I'm ashamed of myself and wonder why God ever let me draw a breath."

"You're pretty tough on yourself for somebody most folks think is a paragon of virtue."

He laughed. "Some paragon I am." The rancor was back in the blue gaze. "Remember, Lane. Don't do anything till you hear from me. I need your word on this. You don't leave town. All right?"

"All right."

He almost never said hello or good-bye.

He just appeared and disappeared. He disappeared now, leaving me to wonder just what he'd heard about Paul that I hadn't.

TWELVE

Over coffee at noontime Callie told me about her morning.

At first, she'd decided against going to school. She just wasn't up to facing the parents who would, inevitably, be at the school door to call her unfit and insist that she resign. Or be fired.

But then she thought about the children. She owed them an explanation and perhaps an apology. She loved them and she knew that most of them loved her. In a very real sense, she saw them as reflections of herself, what she'd taught them these past years.

A group of eight mothers met her at the door. There were no children present. As usual with mobs of any size — and eight is plenty for a mob — there were two outspoken ones. The rest lost a lot of their ire when they saw her. They suddenly felt sorry for her or realized that they, too, had done foolish things in their own past.

Callie tried to get into the schoolhouse to write a note on the blackboard for the students, but the two women wouldn't let her. Nor would they let her get her things out of her desk. Hiram Weaver, one of the two town councilmen who liked Callie and me, showed up and told everybody to calm down. He noted that Callie, whatever her past had been, was a fine teacher and that Skylar was lucky to have her. Callie was heartened by this, thinking that Hiram would at least let her write out her note of apology on the blackboard. But he ultimately sided with the two women and said that it would probably be better if she just went on home for a few days until this thing was all straightened out.

By this time, half the women present were taking Callie's side and arguing with their self-appointed leaders. Callie said that the arguments had gotten not only testy but pretty personal. The only way she could stop the women from having at each other was to slip away. Hiram walked with her to her horse. He was long on apology but short on advice. All he could come up with was: "Maybe you and Lane better stick pretty close to home until things settle down. Grice and Toomey are raising holy hell. Paul's pretty quiet now. He got his way. He somehow managed to get the judge to come up with a sudden case of gout so that Trent couldn't be tried."

She stopped by church and said some prayers. The old monsignor came out. He wore an eyepatch these days because of a detached retina. He emerged from the shadows of the sanctuary, looking pretty damned sinister for a cleric. She'd been almost afraid to speak to him, which was a good measure of how upset she was. He was one of the first people to befriend her when we'd moved here. And now she was afraid of him?

But her misgivings were soon dispelled. He knew that her secret was out. She'd long ago told him in confession of her background, so he was well aware of what she was going through.

"They think I killed him, Monsignor."

"Nobody who knows you thinks that for a minute, child."

"One of the women said that Lane resigned this morning. I've ruined his life along with mine."

"You have to have faith that this will be all right when it's finished."

"But things aren't always all right, Monsignor."

"That's a difficult thing to know sometimes. Even when they go wrong, you see God's terrible wisdom years later. You find out what He really had in mind for you. You see why He made you suffer."

"But Lane's suffering, too." Callie frowned. " 'Terrible wisdom.' That's a strange way to say it, Monsignor."

"Sometimes His wisdom does seem terrible. At least until we come to understand it." He took her slender white hand into his own huge, age-mottled one. "All you can do for now is pray and know that someday, in some way you don't expect, you and Lane will be vindicated."

As she had told Lane many times, the younger priests always had bright little homilies to offer you in times of trouble. It was their way of keeping you and your problems at arm's length — because they didn't have any answers, either practical or theological. They were just human beings.

This was why she appreciated the monsignor's candor. He never offered easy answers. He sometimes implied that righting a wrong might take years, and even then it might not be righted. But somehow the realism of his words was more comforting than the homilies of the younger clerics.

"You have to stand by your husband because he's innocent," the old monsignor had concluded, "and he has to stand by you because you're innocent. That's the strength you have to rely on, Callie. That no matter what they say about you or try to do with you, you're innocent. You know the real truth. That's the only weapon you have. And it'll help you survive this. You'll see."

She went for a long ride afterward. She pretended that she would be teaching again soon. She rode along the river, making note of the various trees and undergrowth and how it had all changed over the course of this lingering Indian summer. She would take her class on a trip. Yes, a morning trip, when the light and the air were at their freshest, and she would identify various botanical splendors for them —

But the fantasy was short-lived. It all came crowding in on her again. She relived her time in the Irish ghetto in Chicago where she'd been raised. Her parents had been loving but frail. She'd watched two of her brothers and one of her sisters die of influenza. Early on she realized that life was a fragile business. She worked in a sweatshop crowded with other immigrant girls, chiefly Jewish. She sewed garments. Though Jews and Catholics didn't especially get along, she made good friends with several of the Jewish girls. For all their seeming differences, both ethnic experiences had been pretty much alike.

On Saturday afternoons, they went to plays together. These tended to be musicales aimed at working girls. They invariably dealt with poor girls being swept away by poor boys who were secretly royalty in disguise — dashing young men who just wanted to see if the girls loved them for themselves and not for their money or status.

The girls, certainly not Callie, never tired of this particular plot. A prince would come into her life someday. She was sure of it. She just hoped it was before she turned eighteen. That was the age when decline began to set in among the girls at the sweatshops. They came in at eleven or twelve, fresh and pretty as morning-cut flowers. But five, six, seven years of working for a dime an hour, sometimes seven days a week, sometimes twelve hours a day . . . well, after a few years of that, who could look fresh and pretty?

So she was all primed to meet somebody like David Stanton that sunny Sunday afternoon when she was strolling in the park with her friend Dorothy Steiner. Dorothy was every bit as pretty as Callie, but she'd fallen in love with a young soldier a few weeks earlier and was waiting for him to get back to Chicago following a brief bivouac for new recruits.

And that's how it happened. Stanton took her to plays, baseball games, operettas in the park. He brought her flowers, candy, even wrote her sweet, corny little poems. He took her to places where she had her first real glimpse of urban society. She didn't know if his friends were really as important as they tried to pretend — but they were certainly more important, and interesting and entertaining, than anybody she'd ever met in the ghetto.

He was wise enough not to even try and seduce her for some time. She was a good Catholic. Her virginity was a very basic part of her entire personality.

But he was sly and he was stealthy and so, two weeks after he'd convinced her to give up her job at the sweatshop, two weeks after he'd convinced her that through his various business enterprises he could support them both, he took her one rainy midnight to his apartment. She'd felt curiously tired and worn that night, sorry that she couldn't be more sensitive and alive to what was going on. Months later, she would realize that he'd drugged her.

Once they were married, she soon realized that his business enterprises were all confidence games. Not only was *he* a crook, so were all his important-acting friends. And even more, he enjoyed cheating people out of their money. He and his friends laughed long and drunkenly into the night, exactly like boastful children, about this or that scam and how much they'd enjoyed pulling it.

She took a teaching job and prayed a lot. Went to three, four masses a week, hoping that God would answer her prayers and turn David into a decent man.

One night, he asked her to deliver some papers to a certain address. She didn't want to, but he berated her enough that she finally gave in. The papers turned out to be forgeries of bank documents. When the mark went to the police, he described not only David but David's "accomplice," Callie. Thus she became a wanted felon. She found a lawyer and instituted a divorce proceeding. And then she fled Chicago before she could be arrested.

"A year later, I met you."

"I appreciate you telling me."

"I've destroyed your life, Lane. I'm sorry."

I shook my head. "I agree with the monsignor. We need to wait and see how this thing turns out. I've got a lot of work to do."

"Work? But you resigned."

"That doesn't mean I can't nose around and ask questions. Besides, I want to see what Edgar's got in mind." I told her about my meeting with Bayard.

"He didn't even give you a hint?"

"No."

"I want to help."

"You can help by writing down everything you did yesterday. Write the times down, too, as close as you can remember them. And mention everybody you saw everywhere you went."

"I don't know if I can. After everything that happened — it's all sort of a jumble."

"Try. You maybe saw somebody who might prove important and we don't know it yet."

She came over and sat on my lap. The rocking chair squeaked. We rocked for a good long time without saying anything. Her head was on my shoulder. The scent of her hair in my nostrils was pretty damned wonderful.

I gave up any hope of relaxing, even here in the rocking chair. I was formulating all sorts of ways Stanton could have been murdered and by who.

I spent the first hour in town getting stopped by people telling me they wished I haven't resigned and that they sure hoped I'd reconsider. I appreciated their words, but at the moment I wanted only one thing and that was to find Ned Hastings.

I had no luck at his hotel, at any of the saloons, at the barbershop or the livery. Hadn't been there.

I walked into the section where the vice was contained. Barbara Parsons ran the most popular of the three whorehouses. The place was open only at night. I found Barbara in the backyard behind the two-story white-frame structure, tending, as usual on a warm day, to her garden.

She was a slender little thing of sixty-some years. She wasn't pretty, but she managed to make herself attractive by dressing in proper Eastern clothes. She had a yellow dress on. A merry yellow ribbon decorated the right side of her graying head. She was using a pink can to sprinkle water on her chrysanthemums.

"Looks good," I said.

"Me or the flowers?"

"You are a flower, Barbara. A beautiful, elegant flower."

"And you are a bullshit artist, Lane Morgan."

I laughed. "My mama taught me to always be polite to ladies."

"Well, then you don't need to worry about me. I've never been a lady in my life." She covered her green eyes from the sun and peered at me. "I heard you quit."

"Yeah."

"I also heard that your wife may be in some trouble."

Enough preamble. "I'm looking for Ned Hastings."

"Then you came to the right place."

I'd expected her to say, at best, that he'd been there and gone. "He's here?"

"Upstairs. Still unconscious from last night."

"I didn't know you allowed sleep-overs."

"I don't usually. But I didn't feel like throwing him in a wagon and hauling his skinny ass back to his hotel."

"What about Richard?" He was her colored bouncer and factotum. "Doesn't he usually haul the unconscious ones away?"

"Richard's a mite indisposed himself. Went to a colored whorehouse in Denver his last trip and picked up a very bad case of the syph. He's back in Denver now bein' treated for it. I sure wish he'd get his ass back here. I need him."

"Mind if I go see Hastings?"

"No roughhousing. I've got a lot of nice

things in my house and I mean to keep them nice."

"I just want to have a little talk with him."

"I hear he's the one who claims your wife killed Stanton."

I nodded. "Stanton ever come here?"

"Just once."

"You talk to him?"

"Not much. He was real interested in Irene."

"Guess I'm not sure which one she is."

"She's new. Little blonde. Looks like she's about thirteen or fourteen. She's actually seventeen. Some fellows like 'em young like that. Seems to give 'em an extra kick for some reason."

"She around?"

"Should be. Turns out Hastings is one of them who likes his pussy young, too. He kept her up till damned near dawn."

"Any trouble with him?"

She smiled. "Not that he wasn't willing to pay for." Then: "Fact, the little blonde tells me he had a nice pocket full of gold pieces."

"Wonder where he got 'em."

She shrugged. "A business like mine, Lane, you never ask. All you care about is if they've got it."

The interior of the house was as tasteful as Barbara Parsons's wardrobe. All very proper furnishings, and a nice big field-stone fireplace in the parlor where the gentlemen sat as the girls came down for inspection. The framed prints were of idyllic New England scenes. Barbara's only visible sentimental streak had to do with her girlhood in Vermont.

Most of the girls were gone. They spent a lot of time shopping. Most folks didn't bother them. There'd been a few incidents, but I was able to get the self-righteous back in their cages before any serious damage was done.

Hastings wasn't hard to find. I followed the noise on the second floor, his snoring. I peeked in on him. He lay on his back, shirtless, in trousers. A few black flies supped on what appeared to be wine. His near-hairless chest was purple and looked sticky.

I went down to the end of the hall, knocked on the door Barbara had told me to. "Uh-huh." That was all the acknowledgment I got. I pushed the door open. She sat in a satin sleeping dress. She was a bit thinner than I liked my women, but she had a face that had probably broken a thousand hearts, all clean-scrubbed innocence just waiting to be defiled.

"Hi, Marshal. I seen you out the window. Talking to Barbara."

I tried hard not to notice her nipples beneath the sheer material. She had a kid grin. "Should I cover up more since you're the law?"

"I'm not the law anymore."

Her fetching blond head gave a start. "How come?"

"Long story. Not worth going through. So I have to tell you that legally you don't have to answer any of the questions I ask you."

She was shining a pair of fancy black shoes, her small hands quick and deft with the rag. "Barbara bought me these here in Denver."

"Nice."

"Comfortable, too." The kid grin again. "You always hear how we spend so much time on our backs. But we also spend a lot on our feet. It's kinda funny how that works out." Then: "So what kinda questions're you gonna ask me?"

"About Ned Hastings."

"Oh." Disappointment in her voice. "He sure does think a lot of himself."

"How so?"

"Big plans. He told me he's gonna have a

gunfight with you and then go into a Wild West Show somewhere."

"What else did he say?"

She shrugged small, pale, erotic shoulders. "He said he was gonna have a lot of money when he left this town."

"He say where he was going to get it?"

"Not really. He started to a couple of times — he was pretty drunk — but then he stopped himself."

"He didn't give you a hint or anything?"

"No. I thought he might. But that's when he started getting sick all the time. I kept running him up and down the stairs. Barbara, she always says get them out the back door and on the grass if they want to puke. She says you stink up a house with puke enough, it always stinks like puke."

"You told Barbara he had a lot of money."

"A lot of money for somebody like him. Near as I could figure out, he's just this drifter with a big mouth and a pretty high opinion of himself. Havin' that much money on him kinda surprised me."

"It surprises me, too."

"When I worked in a Kansas City whorehouse, I spent a night with a couple bank robbers. I was wonderin' if maybe he held up a bank, Ned, I mean."

I kept trying to figure out how old she was. Barbara had said seventeen. If that was true, and she'd already put in some time in a Kansas City whorehouse, she'd sure started young.

"Well, I guess it's time to go pay him a visit."

"He smells pretty bad. I thought of maybe cleanin' him up a little. But when I got in there with a washrag and some soap, he just stunk too bad."

"I'll hold my breath."

That grin again. "You'll need to."

Turned out, she wasn't exaggerating. Ned Hastings was apparently one of those young men who didn't take much to bathing. I got a window open, and then I went over and emptied his boots. A hefty sum of gold eagles fell out, clattering to the floor. His eyelids fluttered. But the noise didn't deter the steady annoying sound of his snoring.

I emptied his gun just as I had yesterday, and then pitched it on the bed next to him. There was tepid water in the bureau pan. I carried it over to him and dumped it on his face. He must have had some night. Not even the water roused him right away. Usually a man would jerk straight up when you woke him that way. He just made some groggy noises and started wiping the water from his face. "What the hell," he said.

"Wake up, Ned."

"Who is it?"

"Sit up and find out."

"How come you poured water on me for?"

"Because I couldn't get you awake otherwise."

"You sonofabitch."

"Sit up, Ned. Now."

"Hey," he said, recognizing my voice. "You're that damned town marshal."

Sitting up was a struggle. Getting his eyes open was even more of a struggle. "Hey," he said once he saw me.

"Hey."

"You sonofabitch."

"You know somethin'? You're almost as aggravating asleep as you are awake."

"What the hell's that mean?"

"It means you snore."

And then he remembered his money. And flung himself on the floor to grab his boot and stuff his hand down inside.

"It's all there," I said.

"It damn well better be."

"Who gave it to you?"

"None of your business."

"Paul gave it to you, didn't he?"

"I don't know no Paul."

I couldn't take it any longer. Or maybe it was simpler than that. Maybe I just didn't want to take it anymore. I was sick of his face and sick of his smell and sick of him. I stood up, walked over to him, grabbed his wet hair, and slammed his head against the edge of the bureau. I slammed it twice more.

"You've been telling lies about my wife, Hastings. That's what Webley paid you to do. If I hear you talking about her again, I'm going to break you up into little pieces."

I gave him a demonstration. I kicked him hard in the ribs. He doubled over.

"You understand?"

He started crying. He sounded young and scared. But there wasn't any pleasure in it for me. At this moment there wasn't any pleasure in anything. My life had been so sweet and uncomplicated since I'd met Callie. And now it had all changed. And maybe it wouldn't ever change back.

There was no sense in talking to him any longer. He knew what he'd done and so did I. Even if he admitted that Webley had paid him to lie, all Webley had to do was deny it.

"You sonofabitch," he said, crying.

145

Irene was in the door. "Gosh, Marshal, what did you do to him?" You could tell she felt sorry for him.

"Not anything half as bad as he did to my wife."

He puked all over himself then, sitting there Indian-legged on the floor, his one boot knocked over on its side, all the gold eagles spilled out like the innards of a cornucopia.

She went over and knelt down next to him and said, "You sure do like to puke." He kept on crying. He was coming off a mighty drunk. You saw men like that sometimes in the morning in the cell we keep for drunks. Confused and ashamed and scared about the night before. They cry like six-year-olds.

I liked her for taking care of him. She was as mercenary as all whores have to be, but she hadn't yet lost all of her tenderness. Kneeling next to him, enduring the stench of his fresh vomit, stroking his head, she could have been his sister or his wife.

From Barbara's I walked back to town. Paul's surrey passed me at one point. He gave me a mocking little nod. Next to him sat his store-window wife looking too severely beautiful to be quite earthly. She didn't give me a nod, mocking or otherwise.

Callahan's was the miner's saloon. It had the least business during the daylight hours of any of the saloons. Its customers were all down in mine shafts. I went there for a beer. I took it to a table and rolled myself a cigarette.

I was just finishing up the beer when Paul Dodson came in. He was the local Realtor. He'd made a lot of money from rich Easterners who liked the idea of having a home in the Wild Wild West. It made for great stories in the drawing rooms as the waiters were serving aperitifs.

"Hey," he said to the bartender. He sounded agitated. "Look outside. They're bringing Callie Morgan in."

He started to say more, but the bartender nodded in my direction. Dodson looked over and said, "Aw, hell, Lane, I didn't see you over there. I didn't mean anything —"

But I was already up and walking toward the batwing doors.

I wanted to see just who was bringing Callie in, and why.

THIRTEEN

I'd had a picture of Callie sitting her horse, her wrists handcuffed, a couple of my former deputies toting shotguns as they rode next to her.

Tom Ryan had brought her in. He rode, without a shotgun, next to our old buggy, which Callie drove slowly down the dusty street to the jailhouse.

If Tom had been showboating, there would have been a crowd. But obviously he had told nobody what he was doing. The only person standing in front of the jail when I got there was Horace Thurman, the county attorney.

He looked embarrassed to see me, which told me a lot. He was another one who had dreams of being a power in the state legislature. I'd done him a favor by resigning. He'd look like a man among men to the lieutenant governor tomorrow. Here was the man who'd seen to it that the murderer was arrested, even though it meant bringing in the former marshal's wife. Surely the lieutenant governor would tell this tale when he once again strode the echoing halls of power. And surely the voters would remember it when it came time to choose their next slate of legislators.

He said, "I'm sorry about this, Lane."

"Paul got to you, did he?" I wasn't in any mood for his slick, empty words.

"You're under a lot of pressure, Lane. I realize that. But that was still uncalled for. I'm my own man."

I sighed, angry as much at myself as at him for the moment. He was many things — overly ambitious, duplicitous, cynical — but he didn't do anybody's bidding but his own. Not even Paul's. Maybe especially Paul's. He seemed to make a point over the years to offend Webley in various ways. Just to prove his independence.

"You're right, Horace. You are your own man. But you shouldn't have brought Callie in."

"You would have brought Callie in. If she wasn't your wife, I mean."

I started to object. But then I realized he was right. I was a long ways from being the perfect lawman, but I did try to do an honest job most of the time. And he was right. If Callie wasn't my wife, she would probably have been my number one suspect.

"What about Sylvia Adams?" I said.

He smiled. "Hard to interrogate dead people, Lane. Maybe you know how to do it, but I guess I never learned."

"Or Ken Adams."

"Tom brought him in earlier. Tom and I questioned him for nearly two hours."

"And decided what?"

"Decided that he was a suspect. But he had a gun on him when he went up to Stanton's room."

"He couldn't have brought a knife?"

"Could have. But unlikely. I asked a few people around town if they could ever remember Ken Adams carrying a knife. They couldn't."

"That's still not very conclusive."

"No, it's not. But the case is a long way from being resolved."

"So now you spend a couple of hours with Callie."

His full face, hidden beneath a trim graying beard, became grim. It was a theater move, one he used frequently in court when he wanted to make an especially serious point to the jury. That didn't necessarily mean he was being insincere. You never know about attorneys and actors. "This isn't pleasant for me."

"She didn't kill him."

"I'm hoping you're right. But if you're not —" His face remained grim. "If I begin to think she really did do it, I'm asking the judge if I can bring in another prosecutor."

"What?"

"We've worked together a good number of years now, Lane. And we've gotten to know each other socially. Callie and my wife are friends. Not intimates, but friends. I just couldn't go after her in court. I like her too much. And in the back of my mind, I wouldn't blame her if she had done it. Stanton was scum. I got a wire from the Cook County District Attorney's office this morning. Stanton was quite a boy. He was even suspected though never charged in three homicides. If Callie did do it, as far as I'm concerned she did civilized society a favor."

I'd been wrong again. All I'd seen when I'd first seen him standing in front of the marshal's office was the ambitious prosecutor about to wade into one of the most notorious trials of his career. But now, if that trial involved my wife, he was stepping aside.

"You want some advice, Lane?"

"I'd appreciate it," I said, barely able to speak after what he'd just said. He was a hell of a lot better friend than I'd ever expected.

"Go up the street and tell Old Sam

Bowen you want him to represent Callie in all this. And then get him to come down here right away. I'll let him sit in on the interrogation. He can make any objections he wants, and then he can spend some time with Callie afterward."

I put my hand out. We shook.

"Since when did you become my favorite person, Horace?"

"You became mine a long time ago. The two of us are the only two who've ever really stood up to Paul in this whole county." He glanced back at the front door I'd walked through so many times. "Well, I guess I'd better get in there. I need to start the questions. And get Tom to buck up a little. He almost handed in his badge when I asked him to go out and bring Callie in. I think it gave him serious doubts about taking the job."

"I'll talk to him. But right now I'll go see Old Sam Bowen."

Bowen, who'd been the county's first attorney, stood out on the boardwalk going through his morning's mail in the sunlight. He was a wiry, bald, nearsighted little man who wore a large Union Army pin on the lapels of all his suit coats. He'd earned several decorations in the war.

I wasn't sure he saw me approach, but

without looking up from a letter he was reading, he said, "You did the right thing, Lane."

"I did?"

"Sure. How the hell could you have stayed on as town marshal with your wife under suspicion that way."

"I guess I did. But some people think I should've stayed."

He laughed. "That's what they say to your face. But behind your back's another matter. If you'd have stayed on, you would have turned just about everybody in town against you."

"You mean people say one thing to my face and another thing behind my back? That kind of shocks me, Old Sam."

That was his name and he liked it. Not Sam. Old Sam. He smiled. "I don't want to hear what people say about me behind my back."

My humor was short-lived. "I need you to be her attorney, Old Sam."

"Where is she?"

"Tom just brought her in. Horace invited you to sit in on the questioning. They're starting any minute now."

He shoved his mail in the pocket of his suit coat. "Then I'd best be getting at it, hadn't I?"

I walked him down to the town marshal's office. He went inside and I went over to where Edgar Bayard had his office. The hitching post outside held the reins of two horses, one of them his. In the street Lem Johnson was scooping up road apples. He was the town's all-purpose hand. "Sorry to hear you quit, Marshal."

"Thanks, Lem." I thought of what Old Sam had said about what people said behind my back.

Bayard's various business interests were run out of a modest office that was hidden among several modest offices on the ground floor of a building that always smelled sweetly of floor-cleaning compound. Nobody else in town used this compound, which was too bad. It had a friendly smell.

I opened the door and went in and nodded to Bayard's secretary, a middle-aged woman whose race had long been a subject of speculation. Though her husband was clearly white, she had a complexion and features that hinted at Negro blood. Some people just assumed that she had brazenly "passed" in white society. I wasn't sure and I didn't particularly give a damn. She was pleasant and efficient.

"Morning, Ruth."

She'd been riffling through a stack of letters. When she looked up, surprise played in her eyes. The surprise was that I was the man of the moment in our small town. A former lawman whose wife, innocent or not, was involved in a scandal. Ruth, a plump woman given to matronly business attire, radiated sympathy for me. She knew what it was like when the gossips focused on you. "Morning, Marshal."

"I saw Edgar's horse outside. I thought maybe I could see him."

"Of course." She stood up. About this time, she'd usually be telling me how good a teacher Callie was. She had a boy enrolled in Callie's classes. This time, she didn't say anything. She knocked gently on the door, opened it, peeked inside, told Bayard that I was here to see him. She stood aside for me. I walked in.

Bayard's office was like the man. Spare and without fuss. A long way from the quietly imposing chambers of Paul's. The pleasant scent of pipe tobacco filled the air. I sat in a plain wood chair across from his plain pine desk. The walls held maps and charts relating to his various businesses.

"I'll bet I can guess why you're here," he said, drawing on his briar pipe. "I just heard they brought Callie in."

"Supposedly just for questioning. She's not under arrest."

"It's that damned Grice and Toomey. And I'm sure that Paul's behind them."

"I don't have any doubt."

He laughed. "We sure wouldn't want the lieutenant governor to think that Skylar had ever had an unsolved murder, now would we?"

"We've got a perfect town here. We wouldn't want to go and spoil it."

He sat back, hooked a thumb in a vest pocket. The pipe stayed stuck in the right corner of his mouth. He talked around it. "So now you want to know what I know — or suspect."

"When you told me about it out at the rail site, there wasn't this much of a hurry. But now that Callie's been brought in —"

"I understand, Lane." He hesitated. "One of my employees saw this. Or thinks he saw it. He was some distance away. And he made me promise that I wouldn't get him involved. All I can tell you is what he told me. It's not proof of any kind. But maybe it would start you looking in a fresh direction."

"That's what I need now. A fresh direction."

He leaned forward. Took the pipe from

his mouth. The last wraiths of his last inhalation wriggled from his nostrils. "You know where Phil Chesney has his cabin?"

"The one he uses for hunting?"

"Yeah."

"Sure."

"Well, you know that Chesney likes the women."

"Everybody seems to know that except for his poor wife," I said.

"Well, he and Stanton got to be drinking cronies. Stanton got a couple of young gals from town here to go out to Chesney's cabin for a few parties. Stanton gave Chesney a perfect cover. If Chesney's wife heard about the parties, all Phil had to say was that he'd let Stanton use the cabin and that the girls were all Stanton's idea."

"And Phil of course would be blameless?"

Bayard snorted. "Well, Letty Chesney's been buying those stories of his for years. So why wouldn't she buy this one?" The pipe went back into his mouth. He dragged on it, but it was already dead. He took a lucifer and struck it underneath his desk. When he got the pipe going again, he said, "One afternoon, this employee of mine is out hunting near the cabin, and he sees Stanton standing on the front porch. And

Stanton isn't alone. Laura Webley is with him."

It sounded right. Maybe it was just because I wanted to believe it. But still and all, it sounded right. "Callie said Stanton used to love to seduce the wives of powerful men. It gave him a sense of power, too. You know, having something like that over them."

"He comes to town and offers all this stuff on Callie to Paul. Webley pays him and asks him to hang around to verify everything if and when it comes out — just in case you didn't back off Trent the way he wanted you to — and so Stanton decides to have a little fun while he's hanging around. He sees that Webley's wife is a beauty and he goes after her. Everybody knows how much she hates this town, thinks we're all a bunch of hayseeds and ruffians, and so when she sees a sharpie like Stanton, she decides to have a little fun for herself." He paused and then said it for me: "What if Paul found out about it? What do you think he'd do?"

"Kill Stanton."

"Right — as far as it goes. But you've got to put yourself in Paul's mind. He's a very devious little man. I admit I hate him because of what he did to the Utes — but I still can't take anything away from him. He plans everything out very thoroughly."

"So," I said, "he kills Stanton, but he also has somebody ready to take the blame."

"And who better than Callie? As I say, you know how much I hate the man, Lane. So my opinion of all this is prejudiced. But I think it's something you should look into."

"Hell, yes, it's something I should look into."

"I don't want to see him get away with this — if he's involved. I'm not going to be alive and kicking too many more years. I'd sure hate to go out with Webley getting away with a murder he'd committed."

"I appreciate this, Edgar."

"I'm the one who's appreciative, Lane. You're doing my work for me. I wasn't sure how to handle this. But I know you will."

"I'm sure going to give it a try, Edgar. I'm sure going to give it a try."

FOURTEEN

I sat in the café across the street from the marshal's office. Callie didn't come out for nearly two hours. Even from here I could see how drawn and shaken she looked. Her shoulders were stooped, which wasn't like her, and when she went to step up on the buckboard, she missed and fell against the vehicle. She put her head down. I wondered if she was crying.

I was next to her in less than a minute, turning her so that she faced me, letting her fall into my arms. She wasn't crying. I held up her face. Her eyes were colder than I'd ever seen them. A kind of crazed cold, part rage, part shock.

Old Sam was there a moment later. "Horace didn't go easy on her. I didn't expect him to. But then I didn't expect him to be quite as rough as he was either." He put his hand on Callie's shoulder. "How you doing, sweetheart?"

"Tired," she said. The anger was waning. She seemed to slump even more. She looked up at me and said, "All the way into town, I kept thinking this was just a formality. That Horace just had to go through the motions. But I think he really believes I did it, Lane. He really thinks I killed David."

"He's taking himself off the case as of right now," Old Sam said. "He's going to send for another prosecutor to handle it."

"I thought he was our friend," Callie said, sounding dazed. "All those dinners at his house —"

Old Sam said, "Maybe you'd better get her home, Lane."

A few minutes later, I was sitting on the buckboard seat, Callie next to me, and we were leaving town. It was a smoky autumn afternoon. I followed the arc of an eagle down the sky to the west and the galloping flight of a chestnut stallion across a hill to the east. Callie said nothing, not even after I told her what Edgar Bayard had told me about Paul's wife.

"How you doing?"

"Tired."

"You go right to bed."

"I really did think we were friends."

"Try not to think about it."

"I'm so sick to my stomach, I want to throw up."

"Want me to stop the wagon?"

"No, please, just go on home."

I got her to bed. I forced her to sip on a shot of whiskey. I left the front door ajar to let in the soft breeze.

"I won't be here when you wake up."

"You going out to that cabin?"

"Worth a try."

"Laura would be just the type David would have gone after. Selling blackmail about me to Webley and then sleeping with his wife on the side. David would think that was just great."

"Sounds like a hero."

She smiled. "Oh, yes, a real hero."

She held her hand up, waved me over to her. I sat down on the bed and put my head into the warm female sweetness of her neck. "It's starting to get loose," she said.

"What's starting to get loose?"

"My neck."

"Not that I've noticed."

"Sure, you've noticed. I'm getting older and my neck's going. That's the first thing that goes in all the women in my family. The neck."

She started crying then. A gentle crying but a very melancholy one. She gets in moods — as do I — when you let it all rush in like a tidal wave, all the things that have bothered you of late, even some of the things that have bothered you for years. And you almost drown in them.

"I just need to cry."

"I know."

"Sometimes it's the only thing I know how to do."

I nodded, held her hand.

"When I get like this," she said, "I even think of the kitten you bought me that time."

"Alexandra."

"Yeah."

"She lost all that weight," she said, "and died so fast. She was so tiny."

Things that have bothered you of late; things that have bothered you for years. Poor little Alexandra was a long ways back there on our road together. But her memory came back to both of us every once in a while.

She took good care of her dun and so did I. I talked to the animal a few minutes, and when he seemed comfortable enough with me, I got ready to go. I used her saddle, a lightweight California style with a lot of tooling, and her bridle, which was braided horsehair. I took her Winchester as well, mine still being back in the livery with my horse.

The warm afternoon seemed to have inspired a lot of work among squirrels, chipmunks, and beavers. I saw a good number of them along the wide lake that led to the steep, rocky Ute path that led to Chesney's cabin. Between the green aspens, I caught glimpses of the ruins some Easterner professors had spent most of the year looking at. The newspaper interviewed them. They said they thought the ruins pointed to a prehistoric civilization of some kind. Callie had read the article to her students. It's all they'd wanted to talk about for days.

The cabin was actually a house and a nice one. Chesney was a minor cattle baron who'd done especially well selling beeves to the Army during the days of the Indian wars. He was an argumentative man, and God help you if you hinted that his prices to our fighting troops had smacked of war profiteering.

The exterior of the place was cedar shingles. There was a long, screened-in front porch. To the right of the house was a gazebo and to the left a horseshoe pit and enough room for a croquet match. He loved his parties, especially the ones his sickly wife didn't attend.

I had no idea what I was looking for.

Even if it was true that Laura Webley had come out here, what did I expect to find that would prove it?

I hid my horse in the woods and then walked up to the house. I had drawn my Colt, though the stillness of the place made me feel a little foolish about it. Maybe I'd have a shoot-out with a raccoon. The place looked deserted.

Before going in, I stood on the porch and surveyed the area. The cabin had been built on the rocky crest of a small mountain. It stood in the center of a clearing surrounded by green aspens and jack pines. You could see sunlit flashes of the lake below. And you could see, in the blue and autumn-hazy distance, the town of Skylar.

The only sounds were those of birds and some heavy thrashing of undergrowth in the nearby forest. Maybe a bear.

I went inside. I always confiscate burglar tools when I find them on felons I arrest. I keep the best of the tools for myself. They come in handy.

The interior of the place was just about what I expected. The heads of a lot of dead animals on the walls — proving the virility of the cabin's owner — leather furnishings, a huge stone fireplace, a polished wooden floor with colorful hooked rugs, a kitchen that most women would kill to own, and a small screened-in porch on the back that was all set up with an expensive poker table and chairs.

The upstairs consisted of three large bedrooms, each laid out identically — bureau, closet, double bed. It all had the feel of a hotel. Everything had been cleaned recently. Even the bedclothes seemed fresh.

I spent half an hour going through all the bureaus and closets and found nothing. I'd come out here filled with hope. I'd find something that linked Laura Webley to Stanton. I'd find something so conclusive that I'd be able to link the Webleys directly to Stanton's murder. And then my wife could have her life back.

I ended up sitting on the back porch at the poker table with the heavy blanket thrown over it to protect it from rain. I rolled myself a smoke and tried to puzzle through what to do next. The trip had been wasted. There'd been a good number of women through this place over the years, but whoever cleaned it up for Chesney made sure there was no trace of them left behind. In fact, the place had been cleaned so thoroughly, it was almost as if no human being had ever set foot in the place.

I was rolling cigarette number two when I heard the sound of horseshoes working carefully against the rocky path leading to the house.

I hurried to the front window to see who was coming.

I'd never seen her in anything less formal than an expensive Chicago dress. Even in a plain white blouse and butternuts, though, there was something formal and doll-like about Laura Webley. Her chestnut hair almost matched the color of her mount.

I walked over to the closet beneath the staircase. Stepped inside, realizing as I did so that she'd find the front door unlocked. Maybe she'd make something of that and maybe she wouldn't.

I waited.

She took some time coming in. I wondered what she was doing. Maybe, finding the front door unlocked, she was leery of walking around inside.

She was as light of foot as Callie. I could picture her diminutive steps, the polite and unimposing way she carried herself, as she stood in the center of all those masculine symbols in the front room — not just the animal heads, but the gun racks and portraits of racehorses and bare-knuckle champions — standing there so elegant and refined even in her riding clothes, seeming a little lost and overwhelmed.

Then she went to work.

She opened and closed all the same closet doors I had, all the same bureau drawers I had, walked all the same steps up and down. And apparently came to the same conclusion I had: Whatever she was looking for wasn't here.

She'd forgotten one closet, though. The one I was hiding in. She knew her way around this place. She'd know where to look and where not to look. I guessed this was one place she ruled out as being a good possibility for her search.

But then, just as I had, she got a little desperate. She started opening and closing some of the same closet doors and bureau drawers again. Second time through. I could imagine her reasoning. *Maybe I missed something the first time through. Maybe it was right in front of me all that time and I missed it.*

I knew that eventually she'd get to the closet I was hiding in and eventually she'd find me.

When the door opened, I just stood there with my Colt pointing directly at her.

She made a small gasping sound and then said, "Oh, God, Marshal, you scared me."

"I meant to," I said, and then stepped out from the closet.

"You meant to? Why, that's a terrible thing to say. And why are you holding your gun on me?"

"I thought maybe you had a gun."

"Me? I wouldn't know how to use one."

"How about a knife? Have you ever used one of those?"

I don't think she understood the implication at first. But within seconds recognition shone in her eyes. "What's that supposed to mean?"

I took her arm. "Where're we going?" she asked.

"The back porch."

"But I —"

"I'll save you the trouble, Mrs. Webley. I've already gone through the whole house. I didn't find nothing and you won't either. Chesney must've hired somebody to clean this place up, and they did a very good job."

She jerked her arm free. "I don't want you touching me."

I gave her a slight shove in the direction of the back porch.

"Paul is going to be very unhappy when

169

I tell him how you treated me."

"He's going to be even more unhappy when I tell him about you and Stanton."

"Me and Stanton? You mean David Stanton? I hardly knew him."

"Sure."

She quit walking. "If that's what this is about, then you'll waste a conversation on me. As I said, I hardly knew him."

"Then what're you doing here?"

"I — I left something here a week or so ago. There was a party."

"I assume Paul was with you. Husbands usually accompany their wives to parties."

For all her beauty and poise, which were considerable, she was an amateur when it came to lying. She gulped and stammered and glanced from side to side. "He was sick. He stayed home."

"I can't think of a single husband who'd let his wife go alone to one of Chesney's parties."

"Paul trusts me completely."

"Then he's a fool."

I gave her another push toward the back door.

When I got her seated at the poker table, she said, "You're not the marshal anymore anyway. Why should I do anything you tell me to?"

"Because if you don't, I go straight to your husband."

"If you mean with that stupid story about me and David Stanton —"

"Somebody saw you out here, Mrs. Webley. Saw you and Stanton."

"I don't believe it. Who saw me? I want to know so I can call them a liar to their face."

"They saw you, Mrs. Webley. I take their word for it. And even if your husband doesn't believe me right away, he'll start thinking about it. He'll start wondering if there wasn't maybe some truth to what I said. And he'll start discreetly asking questions. He's a powerful man. People are afraid of him. Eventually he'll find out the truth. And then where'll you be, Mrs. Webley?"

We didn't say anything for a long time. I just listened to the birds and thought of poor Callie at home. I hoped she was sound asleep. Right now that was the only escape open to her.

Mrs. Webley said, "I only saw him once."

"I don't believe you."

She made a face. Even making a face she was lovely. Spoiled and lovely. Empty and lovely.

"It would destroy Paul. For such a powerful man, he's very sensitive."

"I want the truth."

She sighed. "The truth is I came here today to see if I'd left anything behind. And yes, I saw him a few times."

"You had what the French call an affair."

Her smile was deadly. "Imagine. A town marshal telling me about the French. You've been to Paris, I assume, Marshal?"

"You had an affair. And you started to like him more than you'd planned. And when you found out he was seeing other women, you got angry and smashed up his hotel room."

She started to say something and then fell into silence again.

She had very long, elegant fingers. She splayed them on top of the blanket covering the poker table, and we both inspected them.

She said, not looking up from her hand, "He got mad at me one day when I got jealous, and said that my face and hands were starting to look old. He was lying. He just wanted to hurt me."

She wanted a compliment, reassurance. She didn't get one.

"How many times were you in his hotel room, Mrs. Webley?"

"Just a few times."

"How many?"

She shrugged, finally pulling her gaze from her hands and looking at me. "You know how I got in and out without being spotted? I dressed like an old Indian woman. It was dangerous but it was fun, disguising myself that way. It made me feel young again. Back East — I used to have fun all the time. But out here —" She paused. "I'm sorry I said that about Paris. I was just being a snob. I'm a terrible snob, I'm afraid. It's how I was raised. Then my poor father went broke — he'd owned a huge shipbuilding company and one of his partners betrayed him — and then I wasn't rich any longer. All I had left — all my sisters and I had left — was our totally useless finishing-school education and our snobbery. Those don't get you much in the real world."

"So that's when you met Paul?"

"Yes. He was back East, buying things. He wants to be taken seriously as a person. It's because he's so small. I don't think he feels very manly sometimes. He can't do anything about his size, but he can do something about his social standing. At least he thinks he can. So we go back East two or three times a year, and he buys things."

"You're too bright not to have known what Stanton was right off."

This time there was a sad, knowing warmth in the smile. "Of course I knew what he was right off. That was the fun of it. The danger, as I said. Sneaking around. Having him tell me all those wonderful lies about myself. He hated anybody who was more powerful than he was. So he always made a point of seducing their wives. That way he had the power over them, if that makes any sense."

"Unfortunately, it does."

"But somehow — somehow, I fell in love with him. My God, I can still remember the first time I got jealous over him. I couldn't believe what I felt. I hadn't been like that since I'd had crushes on men at society dances. I even started throwing up sometimes. I'd just get so sick, thinking of him with other women."

She stood up and walked to the far edge of the porch. Pressed her fingers against the screens. "Not even Chesney knew about me."

"Are you sure?"

"I made sure. I convinced David to concoct this story about a girl in her teens he was seeing out here. Chesney would have gone straight to my husband. He's never liked me. At a party once he hinted that we should sneak off somewhere. I was new here. I thought of myself as very proper. I'd never been unfaithful to any of my beaus, and I certainly wasn't going to be unfaithful to Paul. He'd rescued me. He'd made me rich again, even if I did have to live out here. I think Chesney was always afraid I'd tell Paul what had happened, but I never did."

A sudden rustling in the forest. Close by. She jerked around. "What's that?"

"A bear, I suppose."

"What if it isn't?"

"What could it be?"

"A person. Spying."

"Be quiet."

We listened for a time. The noise path of the animal continued through the forest.

"If he's a spy, he's a damned bad one," I said. "Making all that noise."

After another few minutes, the commotion in the woods began to fade. She put her head against her hand and shuddered. "I thought I liked the danger. And I suppose I did at first. But I got tired of it, too. I don't think I'm built for sneaking around. I don't like to think of myself that way. Plus I get scared all the time. Like now, at that bear or whatever it was." She shook her head.

I said, "Did you kill him?"

She watched me. "Do you think if I did I'd tell you all this?"

"Sure. You're telling me all this because you want me to think you're an honest woman. Forthright. Holding nothing back. You could be holding a whole lot back."

"So could you."

"Meaning what?"

"Meaning that Callie killed him and you want to make it look as if somebody else did."

"She didn't kill him."

"I didn't either, Marshal."

"You had a lot more to lose than Callie did. You had a lot of money and a very comfortable way of life to lose."

"Callie had her reputation."

"True. But all Callie needed to do was move with me to another town and we'd start all over where people didn't know she'd been married to Stanton. If Paul divorced you, you'd have to find another rich man to take care of you."

The melancholy smile again. "Oh, I forgot. I'm getting older. Just the way David said I am. I'm losing my charms, aren't I?"

I didn't feel like complimenting her this time either.

She walked to the far edge of the porch, hugging herself as if she were suddenly cold. She stared out at the lawn behind us and the nearby forest. "I'll always remember standing here with him one afternoon. I saw a side of him I thought I never would."

"What was that?"

"This was the only place I ever saw him scared." She turned and smiled at me. "It's a terrible thing to say, but I enjoyed it — seeing him scared."

"What was he scared of?"

"Somebody saw us. Somebody in the woods."

"Do you know who?"

"No. But he was afraid it was Paul. Paul still owed him the second half of the blackmail payment. David was afraid he wouldn't pay it if he found out about us."

I started to tell her about Bayard's employee, then stopped myself. Bayard had definitely said that the employee had seen them standing on the front porch together.

This was the back porch. Somebody in the woods had watched them on the back porch.

I wondered who it had been.

FIFTEEN

On the ride back to my place, I decided it was time to talk to Ken Adams again. There was always the possibility that he — or his wife — had killed Stanton. The same for Laura Webley, too. And now Paul was another possibility. He wouldn't abide another man — particularly a man like Stanton — sneaking around with his wife.

I was on the last stretch of road when I saw Horace Thurman riding toward me. The only place in this general direction was mine.

We met on the road and stopped.

"I was just at your place," he said.

"I kinda figured that. You talk to Callie?"

"Couldn't. She wasn't there." He nodded to my animal. "Isn't that her horse?"

"Mine's still in town."

"You happen to know where she is? I knocked several times but there was no answer. I didn't see any horses so I figured you two were gone somewhere."

178

I knew enough to lie. "The last good pickings for berries. I'm sure she's out gathering them up. Anyway, you just talked to her earlier."

He grimaced. "Lot of pressure from Toomey and Grice. They're working the whole town up. Saying that Tom Ryan and I won't arrest Callie because of our friendship with you. I decided to appease them by riding out here and talking to her again. I wouldn't be surprised if the sonsofbitches followed me. You know how they are when they get a bug up their ass."

"I'll tell her you want to see her."

"I'll stop back later. Toomey and Grice don't seem to think so, but I've got a lot of other cases to worry about besides this one." He laughed. "And whatever you do, remember to wear your top hat and spats tomorrow when you come to see the lieutenant governor. He's going to put on some kind of display for the town. I think Toomey and Grice think he can walk on water."

I nodded good-bye and headed home. I kept the horse at a trot. I didn't want Horace looking over his shoulder and seeing me race home. But something was wrong.

I'm not sure I believe in ghosts exactly,

but I do believe that a mood can settle on a house just like a ghost. I've been in houses where murders were recently committed and you could feel the violence in the air.

I wasn't sure what I felt when I walked inside my cabin. But something troubling lingered there.

I didn't find the note for a few minutes. It was tucked up against the top of the sink. The handwriting was unmistakably Callie's.

Dear Lane,
I've destroyed your reputation and your life. I can't face it. I'm going somewhere far away. I love you with all my heart.
Callie Margaret

I carried the note to the table, poured myself a drink, rolled a cigarette. And just kept staring at the note.

She'd written it under duress. A peace officer gets all kinds of threats, as do his loved ones from time to time. We'd always agreed that if somebody made us write something under duress, we'd sign it with our middle names — Lane George Morgan or Callie Margaret Morgan.

Somebody had taken her.

But who, why, and where?

I searched the house for any evidence of struggle. There was none. But her clothes were gone, as was her suitcase. Whoever'd taken her had done a good job. First by forcing her to write that note. Second by taking all her clothes away. Making it look as if she'd simply run away.

Who, why, and where?

Toomey and Grice would be elated to hear this. There was no better evidence of guilt in a court of law than flight. Now, to all appearances, Callie had run away.

I went outside, found fresh but unremarkable tracks. They could belong to a hundred different horses in the area. The only thing useful was that there was only one set of tracks that indicated two people riding on the same horse. Horace had used the road up and back. The other tracks showed that the rider had approached from over the bluffs to the east and had used the same course.

I got on Callie's horse and followed them all the way down to the river, where I lost them.

I'm not much for sitting around. But I didn't know what else to do. Back at the cabin, I went through everything a second time. I still didn't turn up anything. Her kidnapper had known what he was doing.

In late afternoon, Horace came back. I met him at the door. "Callie back yet?"

"Back and gone again."

A skeptical smile. "This won't do you any good, Lane."

"What won't?"

"Hiding her like this."

"I'm not hiding her. Really."

"Well, she sure as hell isn't out berrying all this time. And since her horse is here — and yours is in town — she's got to be around here somewhere. Mind if I come in?"

"Look, Horace, when she comes back, I'll bring her to you. How's that?"

He dropped all pretext of being friendly. "Lane, you're putting me in one hell of a bind here. Toomey and Grice want her arrested. Tom Ryan won't do it. They're already talking about firing him. And now they're after me to get a confession out of her. They think because we know each other socially, she's more liable to talk to me. I'm arguing that if she did do it, I won't press for anything more than manslaughter. They don't like it, but they'll go along with it. That way, when the lieutenant governor arrives tomorrow, they'll be able to say that law-abiding Skylar locks up its killers very quickly."

"She's not a killer."

"Then if she doesn't have anything to hide, let me come in and talk to her."

"She isn't here."

"Of course she is, Lane. Now please don't make me go back and get a search warrant."

"That's what you'll have to do, Horace. I'm not letting you in otherwise."

He seemed genuinely hurt. "I always thought we were friends."

"Yeah," I said, "so did I. Until you decided that my wife is a killer."

His anger was evident in his blanched face. "I'll be back. And she'd damned well better be here, Lane."

I watched him stalk back to his mount and ride away.

I did some drinking. The effect was neutral. Didn't help, didn't hurt. It was one of the few times in my life I felt helpless.

I watched a rose-and-purple dusk through the window move from the snowy mountains to the aspens and maples on the nearby slope. A deer came all the way up to the open door, peeked in, and then swung away. I gave up drinking and fixed myself a cold dinner.

I went through the cabin again. And found nothing again. I had pretty much decided what was going on. Kidnap Callie, force her to write a letter of confession, and then fake her suicide.

The town would have its murderer. The case would be closed.

Around seven o'clock, I heard a horse approaching. I grabbed my Colt and sat at the table and waited for whoever it was to appear.

I suppose I was expecting Horace Thurman. Instead the man in the doorway turned out to be Old Sam.

"You going to shoot me with that?" he said, nodding at my six-shooter.

"Right now I'd sure like to shoot somebody."

"Guess I can't blame you there. But you wouldn't want to shoot some creaky old bastard like me, Lane. Shootin' younger folks is a lot more fun."

I surprised myself by laughing. "C'mon and sit down."

When he was seated across from me, he said, "You gonna offer me a drink or do I have to sit up and beg for it?"

"I'd like to see you sit up and beg sometime. Hard to imagine."

He poured himself a drink. "Hits the spot."

He wore a cotton shirt and a pair of faded corduroys. He looked like an ancient cowhand.

"I was thinking you'd be Horace," I said.

"Oh, he'll be here, all right. He's gettin' a search warrant."

"Good old Toomey and Grice."

"It isn't just them now. Tom Ryan's doin' his best to hold everybody off — he's the one who'd actually have to arrest you for not cooperating with the law — but he's runnin' out of support. Even the other two fellas on the town council are wonderin' why you won't turn her over."

"Can't, Old Sam. I don't know where she is."

I pushed the note at him.

He read it. "This sure isn't like her."

"No, it isn't. She wrote it under duress." I explained the code of using both her first and middle name. "Somebody took her."

"Took her? But why?"

I explained that to him.

"You seem awful sure about this, Lane."

"I am. She'd never run away. She isn't guilty. Running away is as much an admission that she's guilty."

"They won't believe you. They'll think she took off on her own."

"I know. That's why I'm going to stall them as long as I can. Maybe I can figure out who took her and where she is."

"Then you'd have the real killer, too."

"That's the way I figure it anyway."

He pointed to the bottle. "Mind if I have a few more drops?"

"You just want to make sure it's fit to drink?"

"Exactly right. You're a very perceptive man. I like you a lot, Lane, and I wouldn't want you pouring any bull piss down your throat."

"That's very considerate of you."

He took a whole mouthful of the stuff.

"Horace'll either be out here tonight or early tomorrow morning," he said.

"They want to issue a warrant before the lieutenant governor gets here."

He shook his head. "The man's a fool. I sure don't know why they're making such a fuss over him. He only got elected because he decided to run on the same ticket as the governor, who's a popular man. If he'd run as an independent, the way the lieutenant governor usually does, he wouldn't have gotten ten votes."

"You know Toomey and Grice," I said. "They see themselves as Roman emperors. And they think he can help them."

"You should see all the events they've got planned."

"I'm going to," I said.

"You are? Why the hell would you go down there and let half the town have at you that way?"

I poured a shot for myself and then brought him up to date. "Adams, Paul, Laura Webley — one of them killed Stanton. I just want to see how they react when I show up."

"Grice and Toomey'll try and have you arrested."

"Ryan won't arrest me."

"He's a good man, that's for sure. But you know, he's threatened to resign if they come after you. By the time the lieutenant governor gets here, Grice and Toomey may have their own marshal in place. And whoever that is won't hesitate to move in on you."

"I can't think of what else to do, Old Sam. I want to see those three people close up. See how they look and talk. I've been a lawman a long time. I've developed some pretty good instincts."

He raised the letter, read it again. "That code thing's a good idea."

"Read it in a dime novel actually."

"Thought you hated dime novels," he said in his best sardonic voice.

"We've all got a little hypocrisy in us."

He laughed. "In my case, more than a

little. I'm always talking about law and order, but I've probably gotten a dozen murderers off scot-free in my time. And two of them killed people again. So I'd be willin' to match you any day for hypocrisy."

We talked a good half hour more. He drank coffee instead of whiskey. His papery, gaunt cheeks were flush from the alcohol. He said, "I'd sure think it over hard, Lane."

"You mean about tomorrow?"

"Absolutely. You'll be turnin' yourself over to Toomey and Grice. And they'd just love to make a big show of arrestin' you in front of their important guest of honor. Then he'd go back to Denver and tell them what a couple of comers Toomey and Grice are, forcin' the former marshal to be arrested."

"You know something, Old Sam?"

"What?"

"I agree with you."

"Good."

"But I'm still going tomorrow."

"But why?"

"Real simple," I said. "I don't have any choice."

SIXTEEN

They resembled a small posse: Horace Thurman, Tom Ryan, Toomey, and Grice. I'd washed up in the creek at dawn, and was just putting on fresh clothes when I heard them coming fast down the road. By the time I was in the doorway, they were dismounting.

Tom said, "I'm sorry about this, Lane."

"I know you are, Tom."

"That's a hell of a thing for a peace officer to say," Toomey said. "You're the acting marshal and you're apologizing for doing your job?"

Horace said, "I brought a search warrant, Lane. I'm sorry it had to come to this."

"You're welcome to go inside and look around."

"Are you going to tell us where she is?" Grice said.

"I would if I knew, Mr. Grice. But I don't. When I came home yesterday, she was gone."

"In other words," Toomey said, "she ran away."

"I guess that pretty much tells the story," Grice said.

Horace had the grace to look embarrassed by the two buffoons.

"You want to come inside with me, Tom?" Horace said.

Tom nodded. Glanced at me.

"You're just doing your job, Tom," I said.

"If you apologize to him one more time," Grice said to Tom, "there'll be hell to pay, believe me."

Grice was sensible enough to lean back when Tom glared at him. The glare had the power of a fist.

Horace and Tom went inside.

"You realize you're aiding and abetting a felon," Toomey said to me.

The morning was still fresh. The sun hadn't been up long enough to burn off the dew yet. One of those hazy mornings when it would be nice to float downstream in a canoe and fish a little from time to time. But mostly just take in the splendors of Indian summer on the facing shorelines.

"I didn't aid and abet anybody, Grice," I said. "She was gone when I came home. I didn't know she was going to leave. And she's not a felon. She hasn't been charged with anything yet."

"Well, you don't have to worry about that," Toomey said. "She will be as soon as we get back to town."

They really were interchangeable: stout, loud, preening.

"You could make it easier on both of you," Grice said. "You could cooperate."

"I am cooperating," I said. "I didn't try blocking Horace or Tom from entering, did I?"

"I never did like that sense of humor of yours," Toomey said. "You always make yourself try and sound so superior."

I decided not to respond. Shooting ducks in a barrel is the cliché, I believe.

"There'll be a reward for her," Grice said.

"And that means lawmen and bounty hunters will be looking for her," Toomey said.

"She can take care of herself."

"I can't believe you don't care that your wife ran off," Grice said.

"I do care that my wife ran off. But what the hell can I do about it? I don't know where she went."

Tom and Horace came back.

"She didn't leave a note?" Horace said.

"No."

"Did she mention the possibility she

might take off like this?"

"No, she didn't."

"And you didn't encourage her in any way to take off?"

"I didn't, Horace. Until yesterday I was a peace officer. I'd never advise anybody to run away in the face of criminal charges. I think you know that."

"This is different, Lane," he said quietly. "She's your wife."

"All the more reason not to advise her to run. Grice and Toomey here just pointed out that a lot of people will be gunning for her, wanting the reward."

"What reward?" Tom said.

"We're putting up thirty-five hundred dollars between us," Grice said.

"We're going to announce it when we're on the platform with the lieutenant governor this afternoon," said Toomey.

Horace said, "You two are shameless, you know that? Tom and I are trying to conduct a serious investigation here. And you two keep turning it into a circus."

"She's a wanted felon, isn't she?" Grice said.

"Not yet, she isn't," Horace said. "And even if she was, isn't that a pretty steep reward for what'll probably be second-degree murder? At most. It could easily be manslaughter. Or possibly — since we haven't heard her side of yet it — even self-defense. Stanton was no angel."

Hard to tell which had the most impact on me. The fact that Horace had obviously hardened in his opinion that Callie had killed Stanton. Or that he was open to the possibility that it was self-defense.

"You throwing in with Ryan here, are you?" Grice said.

"I'm throwing in with what's called the law," Horace snapped. "Maybe you should read up on it sometime. It's a fascinating subject."

He turned to me. "I'm going to ask you two questions. And I'm going to trust you to answer them honestly."

I just hoped he'd ask me two questions that I could answer honestly.

"All right, Horace."

"You don't know where she is?"

"No."

"And you didn't urge her to run away?"

"No."

"And I suppose you're going to believe him," Toomey said.

"I'll believe him till you can show me that he's lying, Toomey. Can you show me that?"

"He's got all the reason in the world to

lie, Horace," Toomey said.

"That isn't what I asked you, Toomey. I asked you if you could show me he's lying. You obviously can't, so I'd appreciate it if you'd keep your damn-fool mouth shut."

"I'm counting on your word here," Horace said to me.

"I'm telling you the truth."

Tom said, "Then there's no reason to arrest him."

Both Toomey and Grice seemed eager to respond to him, but kept quiet. Horace's scorn was not anything people wanted to go up against if they didn't have to. He could be as withering out of court as in.

"Let's go back to town," Horace said.

Toomey and Grice shook their heads, but followed him back to the horses. Tom lingered, about to say something to me, thought better of it, and followed Horace, too.

I spent an hour getting ready to head to town myself. But first I was hoping I might be able to break into Ken Adams's place.

SEVENTEEN

When I got there, I saw the oldest girl, Sandra, closing the front door and heading to her horse, which was ground-tied a few feet away. I would've found a place to hide, but as soon as she turned from the door, she saw me. I had to ride up to her.

She was fourteen or so and on her way to becoming as pretty as her mother had been. She wore denims and a blue cotton blouse and her sun-bleached blond hair was in pigtails. "Hi, Marshal." She carried an armload of folded clothes, shirts and clean denims and drawers.

I dismounted. "Hi, Sandra. Is your dad around?"

"He just went on into town. To the mortuary. Mom's gonna be buried tomorrow."

"I'm sorry about what happened."

She paused thoughtfully a moment. "It's a sin to kill yourself. You can't go to heaven when you do that. But the priest, he told us that sometimes God'll let you go to purgatory. You know what purgatory is, Marshal?"

"Yes, I do, honey."

"I bet that's what happened to my mom. Where she went, I mean. Purgatory. I don't think she went to hell. Do you?"

"No, I don't. She was a good woman."

"She shouldn't ought to have done what she did with those men. But she always felt real sorry afterward. I felt sorry for her, the way she'd get, the way she was afterwards."

There was no particular emotion in her words. She sounded as if she might still be having some trouble accepting the fact that her mother was gone.

"Dad says you think he killed that Stanton fella."

Now there was a statement for you. A young girl in all this pain — and I was adding to it by saying that I thought her father was a suspect. "You have to consider everybody who had trouble with Stanton, honey. And that's a number of people, not just your dad."

She squinted into the sun. She had a mustache of sweat beads on her upper lip. Another scorching day. "Then how come you're here?"

"I just thought I'd see how your dad was."

The bright blue eyes grew hard. In this moment at least, she was a lot more woman than girl. "I don't think I believe you, Marshal. I think you think my dad still did it and you come over here to see if you could get something on him."

She glanced back at her horse. That was when I noticed the Winchester in the rifle scabbard.

"I'm not even marshal anymore, Sandra."

This was obviously news to her. She became a girl again, a curious one. "How come?"

"Because some important people in town think my wife Callie killed Stanton. So I had to quit."

"Those important people be Grice and Toomey?"

"Yeah. Pretty much."

"My dad hates them almost as much as he hates Paul." She raised her head and looked at the sun. Apparently she could tell by its position just about what time it was. "I better get back to where us kids're staying. I just come over here to get some clean clothes."

"Well, if he isn't here, I guess I might as well head back."

She eyed me steadily. "He didn't kill Stanton."

I paused and said, "It's good to see you

again, Sandra. And I'm sorry about your mother."

"Maybe she wouldn't have killed herself if you hadn't come out here."

It was funny, and it didn't say much for the instincts I prided myself on, but she was so soft-spoken that I hadn't realized till just then that she hated me. Genuinely and truly hated me. Not only did I suspect her father in Stanton's murder. But I just might have pushed her mother into suicide.

"I've wondered about that myself, Sandra."

"My dad, he thinks you as much as killed her yourself."

"I don't think that's true. Not in the daylight I don't. But I guess late at night when I think about things — I sure hope I didn't push her into it. I tried to get in to stop her, but I couldn't. She wouldn't let me in."

"Maybe you shouldn't ought to have been out here in the first place." She hefted her clothes and walked away.

I wanted to say more, exonerate myself in her eyes — maybe, more importantly, exonerate myself in my own eyes — but all I could do was let her walk away.

I turned my horse toward the road leading to town and headed off. I wanted her to see me go. I didn't want her to suspect what I had in mind.

I rode maybe a quarter mile, then guided my horse into some shallow timberland, keeping in the shadows of aspen and pin oak so that nobody could see me if they were glancing down the road.

When I got near the Adams place, I tied my animal to a tree limb and went the rest of the way on foot, pausing before I walked out into the clearing around the cabin. I wanted to make sure she was gone.

No sign of her or her horse.

The cabin was unlocked. The inside was orderly but poor. The best feature was the plank floor. There were two narrow mattresses piled on each other. I assumed these belonged to the girls. They slept on the floor at night.

The one big room smelled of coffee and whiskey. Adams had done as much drinking last night as I had.

What I was hoping to find was a diary or letters of some kind. A lot of women kept diaries to record what life was like out here. They also wrote a lot of letters back home. And received a lot of letters. Maybe Adams's wife had exchanged intimate letters with Stanton — I knew I was desperate, but I didn't have much choice at this point.

I was just opening the bureau when I heard the cabin door squawk open behind me and a familiar voice say, "I could shoot you right here and right now and tell everybody I thought you was a robber. Seeing's how you ain't marshal no more."

She'd seen through me pretty damn well, Sandra had.

I turned and faced her. Her Winchester led the way into the cabin. "You going to shoot me?"

"You think this is funny?"

"Not at all. I'm nervous, you pointing that repeater at me."

"You should be nervous. You ain't got no right to be in here."

"How about if I just leave?"

"What were you lookin' for?"

"Nothing in particular."

"You think he killed Stanton?"

"I think it's a possibility."

"What if I said *I* killed him?"

"I wouldn't believe you."

"Maybe I was so sick of seein' my ma cheat on him that I killed Stanton myself. You should've seen what it did to him. He'd vomit all the time. And cry. Me'n my little brother'd just hold him, try to help him. But there wasn't no help for him, he loved her so much." She paused. "I wanted

200

to kill her. One night I even took a shot at her."

"I'm sorry you had to go through that."

"So maybe I killed Stanton."

"Maybe you think your dad killed Stanton. Maybe that's why you're telling me all this."

"He didn't."

"He ever hit your mother?"

"Just once. And I honestly think it hurt him more'n hurt her. Afterward, he got drunk and went out to that oak tree to the west and kept hittin' till he broke his hand."

"That was the only time?"

"The only time."

There was still no real emotion in her voice. Flat, just relating facts. You had to read all the misery and terror and conflict into her words yourself. You could hear the kids crying and screaming, and the two adults arguing, both of them trying to understand why she did what she did, cursed somehow in a way neither of them could fathom or do anything about.

"I loved her and I hated her. Sometimes at the same time. And I feel guilty about that now. I shoulda just loved her. She was my mom."

"People can confuse you sometimes."

"You ever loved and hated the same person?"

"Sure."

"It's hell, isn't it?"

And just then, in a way that was both adult and childlike at the same time, her voice quavered and conveyed her confusion and sorrow. And I went over to her and took the rifle and set it down on a table and let her come into my arms. She still didn't cry. She just wanted to be held, and I just wanted to be held, and so we stood like that for just a few minutes, strangers, but comfortable with each other for a tiny clock-strike of time, and then she moved away from me and said, "He didn't kill her, Marshal. I just keep thinkin' of my kid brother. If the law took my dad away to prison — or hanged him —"

There was nothing I could say except: "I don't think he did it, Sandra."

"You mean that really?"

"Yeah. I do." I handed her her rifle. "C'mon, I'll walk you outside. You need to take those clean clothes over, and I need to get to town."

"What's in town?"

"The lieutenant governor," I said.

"My dad says he's a crook."

I laughed. "Your dad is a wise man."

EIGHTEEN

I had to hand it to Grice and Toomey. They had managed to work up so much enthusiasm for Lieutenant Governor Bryce Fuller's visit that at least half the town turned out that sweaty afternoon at the railroad depot. Abe Lincoln couldn't have done much better by returning from the grave.

Miners, merchants, gentry ladies, farm wives, ex-convicts, preachers, noisy children, deaf old men — everybody mobbed the depot platform and the ground parallel to the tracks as the train came churning in.

In the lot adjacent to the depot you saw a similar spectrum of vehicles — fancy surreys, a hansom or two, dusty buckboards, and all forms of bicycles. Even a honey wagon on which adamant black flies the size of knuckles were having their own celebration.

The brass band started playing patriotic songs, and many in the crowd began to sing along. A peacock disguised as a human male conducted the band with a flawlessly florid style that impressed some and made others giggle. I couldn't watch him. It was embarrassing.

One other thing was embarrassing, too. The way people watched me. Another spectrum — this one ranging from the hatred of those I'd in some way offended during my tenure as town marshal to pity from those I'd done right by. Nods, fingers pointing in my direction, whispers. The wearer of a scarlet letter couldn't have been any less prominent than I was in that crowd.

But then the train pulled into the station, deep in so that the caboose came even with the depot doors. The handiwork of Grice and Toomey could even be seen here. The caboose was all decked out in red, white, and blue bunting. It looked like a refugee train car from a political convention back East where the candidates liked to combine politics with aspects of circus.

Even small towns like Skylar attracted nationally known celebrities and speakers as they swept through the West promoting their books or elixirs or controversial beliefs. They were, for the most part, slick, literate, and effective speakers. And they helped banish the old style of Western politician, the sincere immigrant who had simple but sound ideas for local or territorial government and stated those ideas without fuss or subterfuge.

No longer. If you wanted to run for any kind of important office, even a big city local office, you had to be at least half as slick and literate and effective a speaker as the nationally known folks who had been by within recent memory. And the same for your appearance. You had to be all suited up and tidy. And you had to be wily with your gestures and your posturing. You didn't want too much in your speech or your mannerisms; otherwise you'd look like the band conductor. On the other hand, you didn't want to stand up there and mutter and mumble and look cowed. One of the state newspapers had even said that a few of the major state politicians had hired the services of drama teachers to help them perform better on the stump.

Whatever else he was — a man of empty words, a man with an open palm for anybody who wanted to lay greenbacks on it, a man who had proved useful to just about every sinister vested interest in the state — Bryce Fuller was a talented performer. He had the looks for it, that rocking-chair-on-the-porch white-haired amiability of grandfathers everywhere; the frank, blue-eyed gaze of a man you could trust; and teeth so damned white they could blind you if he chose to smile into direct sunlight. He was big but not fat; handsome but not pretty; well-dressed but not dandified. The women loved him, but their husbands didn't have to worry about him trying to get into the knickers of either wives or daughters.

Within two seconds of the caboose coming to a stop — the locomotive all scorching steam and hot oil and searing steel — Grice stood on one side of Fuller and Toomey on the other.

The band was ear-numbing in its fervor now; so was the crowd. It applauded, whistled, stomped. It sang, it screeched, it screamed. An arthritic old man, perhaps insane, broke out into some kind of jig. A matronly woman, dazzled by the sight of Fuller, touched her bosom in a most suggestive way. And a man blinded in that long-ago blue-gray war of ours had tears streaming down his cheeks. I could not tell you why.

Frenzy. That was the only word for it. And Grice and Toomey were swollen with the moment even more than Fuller, who had probably had so many moments like this that they'd become routine, maybe even a little dull.

It took Fuller several moments — looking humble, his entire body saying, *Please, please, I don't deserve all this; wonderful and special and godlike as I am, I am just like you, just another human being, well, maybe just a wee bit more wonderful and special and godlike than you, I guess, I have to humbly admit* — it took him several minutes before he finally calmed the crowd and spoke.

"I was saying to the conductor as we were pulling in, 'I believe this is the prettiest town in the whole state,' and he said, 'Yessir, I believe it is.' "

Raptured applause.

"And I'll tell you something else your beautiful town is and that's lucky — lucky to have two men as devoted to Skylar as they are to their own families. And I'm talking about the men on either side of me at this very moment." He introduced them. They looked like children who'd just been given a gold eagle to spend on candy.

"And something else that conductor told me. He said that my friends here — these very two men next to me — were the only ones brave enough to stand up to a town marshal whose wife may or may not have something to do with a very unseemly murder. The conductor told me that not everybody was happy when these two gentlemen forced him to resign — but that they stood their ground and are now in the process of finding his wife."

The applause wasn't rapturous this time, but it was solid. And it inspired a hundred arrow-perfect glances back at me where I stood near the rear of the depot.

"You know what we call that kind of courage in the state capitol, don't you? We call it leadership. The courage to do the right thing even when it's not always popular. The courage to stand up — even if you have to stand up alone — and say that what's right is right and what's wrong is wrong. That's leadership, as I say.

"And I say one more thing. Your district will have two open seats in the state legislature next session. And I can't think of two more qualified public servants than these two gentlemen to fill those seats!"

The band conductor — who had no doubt been silently cued from the caboose platform by Grice or Toomey — broke into another patriotic medley. There was confetti. There was rapturous applause again. I'd been expecting the political push for Grice and Toomey to come later. But he'd probably been asked by Grice and Toomey to make it right away before the crowd started getting tired of the heat and began drifting away.

And then I saw them.

They drove the fanciest surrey of all. And came late, as always. Lateness signified their importance. Courtesy wasn't necessary when you were among the elite. You ran on your schedule, not anybody else's.

Laura Webley, in a summery yellow frock with a vast straw picture hat tied under her chin with a matching yellow ribbon, stepped down from the surrey with storybook grace. Any number of men in the crowd, much to the displeasure of frowning wives, turned to where the surrey had parked very near the tracks — nobody else had been allowed to park this close — and where Laura was making her first public appearance of the day.

Paul helped her down, of course. He looked shrunken and gray standing next to the fully bloomed and life-pulsing wife of his.

"Ah!" Fuller said. "And here come two more very good friends of mine now. Do you mind if I tell you how beautiful Laura looks today, Paul?" The first hint of the lecher in the grandfatherly visage.

Paul pointed gallantly to his wife the way

an impresario points to his diva, letting everybody drink in the elixir of her beauty.

Fuller had misstepped, and from the look on the faces of Grice and Toomey, they knew instantly that he had. In a town like Skylar, a powerful man like Paul is feared and catered to. But he's never liked or admired. Quiet and modest as he could sometimes be, Webley constantly flaunted his most valued treasure — his wife. And she was the embodiment of all that the town resented about Webley. She was too beautiful, too well-bred, too pampered. Only a rich man could catch a woman like Laura — if he wasn't rich, she would've laughed at him the first time he approached her and flounced away. So it was not wise for an invited guest to dote on this woman, nor the man who kept her in his eye.

He'd misstepped but he was good, Fuller was, and realized his error instantly. The faces of the hardworking citizens of Skylar weren't all that hard to read.

He changed subjects deftly. "And let's not forget that beauty comes in many forms. From here I can see all the new buildings in the business area that my friends Toomey and Grice helped build. You Skylar folks should be very proud of your town."

Now what kind of crowd wouldn't applaud a line like that? The Webleys were all but forgotten as Fuller picked up the pace of this speech he'd given so many times, substituting only the name of the town. Even in a hellhole like Leadville, an ugly scourge of mining and anti-union violence, Fuller would be fully capable of talking about "beauty" and civic pride.

Eventually, people quit staring back at me. Picnic tables had been set up in the park, food of every sort filling them. The band led a march to the park, a good portion of the crowd following it merrily along. It was a day for kids, dogs, young lovers — and local political powers who had their eyes on the state legislature.

There was one man I wanted to see before I looked up Adams. There was a problem, however. Paul was surrounded by a gaggle of toadies in fine summer clothes. Getting to him wouldn't be easy.

But then the lovely Laura helped me out by breaking away from the crowd and walking over to where Fuller stood, shaking hands with another group of toadies. The common folk had done the sensible thing. They'd headed over to the food and the beer. Who wanted to stand before would-be greatness and have to genuflect in this punishing heat?

Laura knew better than to force her way up to Fuller. She stood in line. But not for long. I went over to her and took her arm and tugged her away.

"Paul's not going to like this," she said. "He's watching us right now."

"That's the idea. I want him to come over here."

Fear filled her eyes. "What're you going to do, Marshal?"

"Ask him a few questions."

"You're not going to tell him about Stanton and me, are you?"

I started to answer her, but it was already too late. Paul already stood next to us. "Well, Lane, I'm a little hurt you didn't invite me to this little palaver. Being's as how I'm Laura's husband and all. And I don't appreciate you taking her out of a receiving line against her will."

"You sure it was against her will?"

"Of course it was against my will," she said.

"I guess that settles it, Marshal," Webley said. "Now, if you don't mind, Laura and I have some other things to do."

He took her arm and started away.

I said, "About half an hour ago I wired the state attorney general and told him that you tried to blackmail me into dropping charges against Trent."

Maybe it was just the heat, maybe it was just the fact that he'd always found me a nuisance, maybe he was just showing off for his wife, demonstrating that he didn't have to abide people like me.

He spit in my face. The spittle burned unnaturally. It was the humiliation, of course. My instinct was to smash his face in. But I had too much to do to risk going to jail. And Webley had the wherewithal to put me there if he wanted to. If Tom Ryan wouldn't do it, Webley would simply buy himself a lawman who would.

The remnants of the crowd had been idly watching us, waiting their turn to shake Fuller's hand. They were well aware that Webley and I were old foes, so keeping an eye on us might have its rewards.

They gaped, they gawked, they smirked, they simpered. We'd given them — or Webley had anyway — a nice, nasty little story to recite and contemplate for the rest of the day. They were too far away to know why he'd spit in my face — which would just make all their speculation that much more fun.

Hey did you hear about Webley and Morgan getting into it at the train depot?

Man, I thought Morgan might draw down on him for a minute there —

I reached in my back pocket and took out my handkerchief and wiped the spittle away. And then, with a hand I couldn't control, I slapped him with enough force to knock him into Laura.

Now the onlookers would really have something to talk about. The only thing better than a slap was an outright gun battle.

The crowd was ready for a few of his boys — who always hovered within easy distance of him — to move in on me. This was the stuff of local legend. Somebody slapping Paul. When the story was told — and it would be told and retold as long as Paul was alive, and maybe even longer than that — the fact that he'd earned my slap by spitting on me would be forgotten. All that would be remembered was my slap. And what a brave man I'd been. That's the trouble with legend. It always forgets to include the important details. I hadn't slapped him because I was brave. I slapped him because he'd pissed me off and for a moment my temper overruled my good sense.

So what was it to be? His boys moving in on me now or later?

Certainly, Paul couldn't accept the public embarrassment of being slapped by a defrocked town marshal, could he?

But he surprised me — and I'm sure the onlookers — by quietly saying, "I'm sorry, Morgan. I shouldn't have spit on you." He touched the cheek I'd slapped. "I had that coming."

He took Laura's arm again and led her away. Both of them kept their heads down, not wanting to meet the eyes of the gawkers.

Then Toomey was there. "I suppose you're proud of yourself."

"I'm not ready for any of your bullshit, Toomey. It's too hot."

But he wasn't finished scolding me. "We invite the lieutenant governor of the state — one of the most important men in the entire West, a very good personal friend of the president of the United States if I need to remind you — we invite him here and what do you do? You start an argument with one of his very best friends, Paul. You know what he said? He said he wasn't surprised that you were the town marshal who's hiding his wife from everybody. He said that the West is changing and that there's no room for corrupt peace officers like you anymore. And you know what,

Morgan? He's exactly right. Exactly right. You know and I know that that wife of yours killed David Stanton. And you'd damned well be ready to turn her over. Because we're going to double our reward after your disgraceful run-in with Paul this afternoon. We're not going to let you get away with anything, mister. Not one damned thing."

The male schoolmarm had just upbraided me in the harshest way possible. I was going to have to stay after school every day for the next six years, probably, the kind of trouble I was in now.

I was done with him. He might not be done with me. But I was done with him. He started yammering again, but I just turned to my left and walked away. He even shouted at me, but I didn't care about that either. Just headed toward the business district, where I definitely had some business.

Sometime in the middle of the night — one of those nights when you sit on the edge of your bed in your underwear and keep rolling cigarettes — you remember something that strikes you, in the early morning darkness, as something you should've followed up on long before now.

The time was nearing four o'clock.

The night shift would be starting at the hotel.

There was a man there who might just know who'd killed David Stanton.

NINETEEN

Raymond Gunderson lived on the first floor of the hotel where he worked as night clerk. I knew this because I'd been called to his room one night to break up a poker game that had turned into a fistfight. One of the losing players — a hotel guest — had accused Gunderson of cheating. One of Gunderson's friends had held the man while Gunderson started to work him over. What Gunderson hadn't known was that the man was a former boxer. He beat up Gunderson and his friends pretty badly, destroying the room and waking up half the hotel's guests in the process.

I waited in the alley behind the hotel until I saw it was four o'clock. I went in the back door, went down a long, narrow, shadowy hall that opened on the lobby. Gunderson was just getting set up for his four-to-midnight shift. He was studying the guest register and spritzing the air with some kind of flowery-smelling water. As usual, he managed to look both prissy and sinister, no small accomplishment.

I didn't let him see me. I walked back to his room.

A couple of new guests were just coming in the back door, toting heavy boxes. Drummers bringing in some of their wares from a wagon in back. Breathless, sweaty, they still had their dead bright smiles in place as soon as they saw me lingering in the hall. They'd be smiling those empty smiles when they were six feet under.

The third skeleton key worked and I was inside.

I hadn't known that Gunderson had been married or that he'd had a daughter. He had photographs of his wife and child everywhere. I didn't like that. It made him human to me, and that's never a good thing when you're about to rattle a man for information.

The room had that lonely air particular to rooms of men without women. The years pass and all they have to show for it are a few extra dollars from poker, bad lungs and bad heart from too much liquor and tobacco, and the silent regrets seen on the faces of loved ones they deserted long ago and far away. When they're buried, these men, their funerals are attended only by other unmarried men like them. And probably even before the last shovel full of dirt thrums against the lid of the pine coffin, a new unmarried man will have moved into the dead man's room, with his own set of photographs of the family he left behind, and his own air of just marking time before a bullet or the cancer or some odd freak accident claims his body and his soul.

I wondered if I'd end up in a room like this some day, marking my own time.

I went to work. It didn't take all that long. I looked in all the obvious places — dresser, closet, under the mattress, under the bed — and then I noticed the expensive pair of riding boots stuck in the corner by the chamber pot. I figured maybe it would be in the boots, but when I picked them up to look inside, I nudged the pot and noticed that it didn't rock back and forth the way such a light piece of metal normally would.

Despite its odor, I picked it up. Slid my hand along its bottom, which was made of felt and was far thicker than I was used to seeing.

I took my pocketknife out and jimmied the felt free from the bottom of the pot itself. Five hundred dollars fluttered to the floor. Pretty decent pay for a night clerk.

I stuck the money in my pocket and left the room.

I sat in the lobby for the next half hour. Reading magazines. Rolling cigarettes. I was tempted to head into the taproom for a beer, but then I might miss my chance. I needed a few minutes when Gunderson was free, no guests around at all.

When the time came, I was on my feet in seconds, headed directly to the desk.

Gunderson eyed me scornfully and said, "I'm told you made a fool of yourself at the depot this afternoon."

"That's one thing you should know about, Gunderson, making a fool of yourself. You do it all day long."

He sighed. "What can I do for you, Morgan? I'm busy."

I had no proof of what I was about to say, but I had a pretty solid sense I was right. "You a good friend of Webley's, are you?"

"Is that supposed to mean something to me? Of course I'm friendly with Webley. In case you hadn't noticed, Morgan, the man you slapped this afternoon runs this town."

"It's funny. When I picked up your chamber pot this afternoon, five hundred dollars fell out. Only man I know who could put out that kind of money would be Webley."

He leaned forward so he could hiss at

me. "What the hell were you doing in my room?"

"I just wanted to see how much he paid you to keep his little secret."

He leaned back, righted his posture. "I'm sure I don't know what you're talking about." But he was sweating suddenly, and I didn't think it was the heat. He took his handkerchief from his sleeve and began daubing his face with it.

I took the money from my pocket and showed it to him. "I thought I'd let you know I have your money. In case you want to report it stolen, I mean."

His eyes flicked around the lobby. He was obviously afraid somebody might hear us.

"That's my money, Morgan."

"Not anymore, it's not."

"I need it, you bastard. I've got some bills I need to take care of."

I smiled. "You're a lousy gambler, Gunderson. You should've quit a long time ago." I thought of the pictures in his room. "Or stayed with your family. Your wife looks very nice and smart."

"I want my money." He put his hand out, palm up.

"He snuck up the back way, didn't he? And you saw him. And he knew you saw him. And later he came down and told you not to tell anybody you'd seen him go up to Stanton's room. That's why he paid you the five hundred dollars. Or maybe it was more. Maybe you've already spent part of it. Keeping the gamblers off your back. Before one of them shoves a knife in that back because you owe him so much money."

"You don't have to worry about that," he said. And for the first time, I saw sorrow in his face — middle-aged sorrow, lonely-room sorrow. Scared and confused. And then I felt the same as I had when I saw his family pictures. I didn't want to see his sorrow. I didn't want anything to make him human. I had a sense now of why he'd left that nice little family of his. Not a woman. Not the promise of gold. Not an idle dream of power.

No, he'd left because something happened to him when he gambled. Some rush of excitement, some thrill even more powerful than money itself. Gambling had an almost sexual grip on him.

"He's going to kill you, you know," I said.

He leaned forward, spoke in a low voice. "You don't understand, Morgan. That isn't why he paid me. He came here —

snuck in — to get his wife. He paid me to keep quiet about her, not him. He didn't have much luck. He almost ran into Tom Ryan, who was looking for that con artist who'd been in town. Conroy. You know the one. Webley had to hide in an empty room. Then he went in and got her and got out of here fast. I went up there and looked in Stanton's room and — He was dead."

"You think she killed him?"

He shook his head. "That's all I'm going to say."

The door opened. A trail-dusty man in a good suit came in with a carpetbag and a pint of whiskey he would no doubt consume in his room tonight.

I slipped Gunderson his money and walked to the front door. Five men stood there waiting for me. A somewhat embarrassed-looking Tom Ryan; Toomey and Grice; and two deputies I'd hired once upon a time.

Pretty easy to figure out what was going on. Toomey and Grice wanted to use this opportune moment to demonstrate what law and order meant in Skylar.

They'd arrest me in a public way. And drag me off to jail — aiding and abetting; not cooperating with an official investigation; resisting arrest, they'd come up with something — and then post a couple of armed guards out front as if I was Billy the Kid and the Dalton gang combined. Toomey and Grice knew how to do things like this.

I moved swiftly down the interior hallway to the back door. I knew even before I got there what I'd find. Another armed deputy. Waiting for me.

I took the back stairs two at a time. When I found a silent room on the second floor, I pushed open the door and went inside with the help of my skeleton keys. An older gent lay on his back, snoring beneath a book that had dropped on his face in sleep. There was a damp, wild, but satisfied sound to his snoring. He didn't wake up the whole time I was in there.

I had remembered correctly. The building adjacent to the hotel was a one-story structure. I pushed up the window, crawled up on the sill. Toomey and Grice and the lawmen couldn't see me from this angle. Neither could the deputy in back.

As the man continued to snore, as the town moved toward dusk's festivities — there were to be fireworks and a band concert and another picnic spread, and of course the guest of honor was going to favor us with another of his self-serving sermons — I made my move.

Jumping wasn't going to be all that easy for me. I'd inherited the family curse of arthritis. And there was enough of a divide between the two buildings to make landing somewhat uncertain. Halfway there, I could plunge to the ground. I'd certainly break something, a leg most likely. They wouldn't have much trouble finding and arresting me then.

I glanced over at the dozing man. Sure looked enviable, lying there that way, enjoying himself in the comfort and safety of his little world.

I looked back at the roof below me.

I jumped.

TWENTY

My first sense was that I'd sprained my right ankle. I hadn't exactly landed with any skill or grace.

But when I stood up on the pain, it started to go away. I'd stunned my ankle, not sprained it.

The dusk sky gave me just enough darkness. People would have a difficult time seeing me. I moved to the rear edge of the roof. In the first faint moonlight of the evening, I saw the eyes of a couple of prowling tomcats as they searched the alley for food. Scraps of human food would be fine — there was a café on this block and cafés were the preferred hangouts for such cats — or mice or rats. Cats, despite their reputations for being finicky, just weren't all that choosy.

There was a delivery buckboard in back. The bed was high enough that I could drop into it without hurting myself. I didn't want to drop all the way to the ground.

By now I had my gun drawn. I wasn't taking any more chances. I had no desire to be put on display by Toomey and Grice.

I took it easy this time, turning around, grabbing the edge of the roof, and easing myself down backward into the delivery buckboard. No chance of spraining anything this way.

Then I was on the ground and moving as quickly as I could through a series of dark alley passages to the livery. I hid behind a tree to the right of the place till I could find out where the night man was. After a few minutes, he came out of the livery and joined a small group of folks standing in the street. They were all laughing and smiling. Ready for the band concert and the free food.

I went around back, found my horse, saddled him quickly, led him quietly down the alley. I didn't jump up into the saddle until we were a good block away.

Forty minutes later, I was home.

All the way out there I kept thinking she was going to be there when I got there. And not only would she be there. Tom and Grice and Toomey would come along soon after and tell us that Laura Webley had confessed. And then life would be the same again. I'd get my old job back.

She wasn't there. Neither was Tom or Grice or Toomey.

I fed the cat, took my Winchester down, put on dark clothes, and poured myself a judicious belt of whiskey.

I sat in the front door rolling one cigarette after another until full starlight turned the landscape into a place of silver-tinted shadows. The sharp, solemn cry of a night owl signaled night's dominion. All I could think of at first was Callie. Where she was. How she was. She hadn't run away. I was sure of it.

Laura Webley was the killer. Of that I was now certain. But how did I get to her? Or did I get to her? Maybe it made more sense to challenge Tom himself. Somehow, I had to get into the Webley compound and make one or both of them confess.

I knew I couldn't stay here long. Despite a certain weariness, I had to push on. There would be a posse here soon. All for the amazement and amusement of our esteemed lieutenant governor. Any other time, I doubt Toomey and Grice would've moved quite so quickly. But now, if they couldn't get Callie, they'd get me.

I grabbed my Winchester and fled.

TWENTY-ONE

Abe Lincoln once said that if a man wants to kill you badly enough, he will. Unfortunately for Lincoln, he was right. I'd always looked at his remark from his point of view — from the eye of the pursued rather than the pursuer.

But now I was the pursuer.

The ride to the Webley spread took nearly an hour. The temperature kept dropping. I wished I'd worn a jacket.

Webley, at the insistence of Laura, had built a Victorian house that would pass for a castle until the real thing came along. In the stark moonlight, its turrets, spires, and soaring center section resembled a storybook structure. The only thing missing was a moat. Men in chain mail riding fire-snorting golden steeds would likely come pouring across the moat bridge any moment now.

I'd been out here a few times on business, that business usually involving some trouble with young Trent. I knew the general layout of the first floor of the house's interior. And I knew where the guards would be now in the shadows.

I decided the best way to come in was from the southwest. If things were as they'd once been, there'd be a perimeter man there with a shotgun. Webley's men wore khaki uniforms not unlike those of law enforcement's. He liked things official-looking.

The trick would be distract the guard, then take him out in some fashion. The difficulty was getting close to him without getting shot. I wasn't town marshal any-more. He wouldn't have any hesitation about shooting me.

Dusty grass, silvered by moonlight; the rim of a forest cast in deep shadow; oil lamps burning in half-a-dozen mullioned windows. This was what lay before me as I approached from the north.

I considered but rejected the ancient Indian trick of coming in fast on your horse, rider concealed on the far side so it looked as if there were no rider. Webley's men knew all the old tricks. And a lot of newer ones I hadn't heard about yet, I was sure. He hired them cold-blooded, not stupid.

The fire was the best idea, I decided by the time I'd swung wide and come out near the forest. There was a small white gazebo far from the main house. It sat in the middle of a sea of buffalo grass about ten feet from a wide, clean creek.

But it was close enough that the guard would investigate it himself before he'd call out for help.

I spent twenty minutes in the woods putting together just the right amounts of dried foliage, twigs, and paper as a means of starting the fire. The paper I got from my saddlebags, a small catalog offering various kinds of fancy law-enforcement gear that I hadn't had a chance to look at yet.

If I took a direct run at the gazebo, the guard would likely spot me. That meant taking the creek. I could get right to where the gazebo was. This would cut way down on the chances of my being spotted.

I had four lucifers. I should have brought more, but I hadn't thought to check. The only thing that could stop me now was if I couldn't get the fire going in four attempts.

I ground-tied my horse and got to it.

The creek was a good three feet deep in places. It smelled fresh and cool. But the red clay banks were at best two feet high. I had to crawl on my hands and knees, and even then I didn't feel sure that the guard couldn't spot me.

I started crawling up near the woods. If I

slipped into the creek any later, I was afraid he'd see me right off. It seemed like hours passed before I came within sight of the mansion. I cut my hands on sharp rocks. A couple of times, trying to keep hunched down, my feet slipped into the water, which was a hell of a lot colder and wetter than it had any right to be.

I kept the Victorian spires — exotic-looking played against the moonlit sky — in constant view so I had some sense of progress. My left hand was filled with all the material for setting the fire.

And then the snake was there.

Now, I'm not particularly afraid of snakes. Don't especially like them, but certainly don't get all sweaty and nervous when somebody brings up the subject of reptiles. Or I see one for myself.

But given the conditions — the night, trying to keep my body from peeking up over the edge of the creek bed, worried about how I was going to get into the mansion — I was really startled by the damned thing.

It was a milk snake. That kind of gray, coiled, slimy thing you mostly see around dairy barns. But you see a pretty good number of them around creeks in summers, too. They like to sun themselves.

It had been sleeping under a rock, presumably in or near its hole, when my hand nudged the jagged stone and the snake struck my hand.

Milk snakes aren't poisonous. Even their bite is pretty minor. But given the night, the moment, the thing scared the hell out of me.

I didn't scream. I wasn't that surprised by it. But what I did do was jerk upward and then roll down into the creek, so that everything from my hips on down was in the water.

I realized instantly what I'd done. The lucifers were in my left-hand pocket. I'd managed to keep the foliage and paper dry. But what good was foliage and paper if you didn't have a match?

I jerked my body from the water and immediately shoved my hand into my pocket. Brought up the lucifers.

I held them one at a time up to the moonlight, held them up no higher than the creek bank, of course.

Two of the matches were soaked. I tossed them away. Of the remaining two, one match head was damp on only one side. The other lucifer looked and felt dry.

My chances of starting a fire were down to two — at best.

At least I'd managed to keep the paper and kindling dry.

Now for the first big risk, getting from the creek to the gazebo without being seen. I slowly raised my head until my eyes were level with the grass. From this angle I could see the gazebo and a good piece of the south side of the mansion. I didn't see the guard anywhere. Was he walking around? Had he seen or heard me and decided to ambush me? Was he lying in wait on the far side of the gazebo?

I had no choice except to find out. I crawled up over the bank, my soaked pants feeling like worms against my skin. I realized then that I'd forgotten to check my Colt. A bit of it had been in the water. Would it fire properly? Sometime tonight, I was sure going to need it.

When I reached the halfway point to the gazebo, I saw him. The guard. He'd been far back in the shadows of the house. He now stepped into the moonlight and began his sentry duty of walking up and down his quadrant of the property. As soon as he turned and began walking, I dug in my elbows and started crawling even faster for the shelter of the gazebo.

The octagonal-shaped structure had steps on both sides. The problem was that the steps would expose me to the guard again. If he was standing in just the right place, he'd have no trouble seeing me crawl up and inside. The other problem was that I wouldn't be able to see him while I was crawling up those steps. I'd just have to hope that he wasn't within sight.

I took a huge gulp of air and worked my way up the three steps. I couldn't see the guard from where I was. That didn't rule out the possibility that he'd seen me. He might be sneaking around in back of me right now.

I got myself up into a crouching position. The gazebo interior consisted of a pewlike seat that stretched all the way around the interior wall. Dark red cushions covered the wood. Here and there you could see books and newspapers. Apparently, people came out here to read sometimes.

I angled myself away from the two entrance points so that I could set up the fire. It had been years since I'd started even so much as a campfire. Trains and stagecoaches had spared most people from traveling long distances on horseback. And camping out every night on gassy beans and tooth-jarring hardtack.

The first match, the one damp on one side, sparked for a moment, but then the match head itself disintegrated, first the wet side and then the dry, but cracked, other side. The flare had lasted no more than a moment.

I crawled over to the edge of the entrance and dared a peek for the guard. He was back in place — though not lost in the shadows this time — and at the moment stoking up a cigarette.

Given the fact that I had only one match, and given the fact that it might misfire and leave me with no fire, I decided to see if there was some way I could sneak up on the guard. I thought that maybe from a different angle —

But no. No matter how sly I was, he'd see me. And shoot me.

I haunched backward and decided to try my luck again with the fire.

I fixed up alternating layers of foliage, paper, and broken pieces of dry wood. Then I took a sheet of paper and rolled it tight. If I got it to light, I wanted it to last awhile, as near to a candle as I could make it.

A coyote; a dog; a piano played suddenly inside the house.

A breeze, too chill on my wet legs; a smell of whiskey and cigars from some happy moment here in the gazebo; a couple of cigarette butts on the floor.

I held the match close to my eyes. From what I could see, it looked perfectly fine. A good old reliable match. But what if it wasn't? But there was no point in thinking that way. You get to a moment when thought doesn't matter. Only action does. And there's a kind of wary thrill to that moment. Your fate is in the hands of the gods and you can never outguess them, not ever.

I closed my eyes, the way I did when I threw dice. I didn't want to look. I wanted to open my eyes and be surprised. A good surprise.

I struck the match on the dry wood floor of the gazebo. I could hear the sizzle when the flame came up, feel the heat sear my fingers.

When I opened my eyes, the flame was burning true. I set it against the sheet of paper I'd rolled up tight. It ignited instantly.

I leaned down and touched the paper to the fire material I'd prepared.

That's when it went all to hell.

The stuff I'd gathered wouldn't ignite. I wondered if it had been sprayed with creek water and I just hadn't noticed it.

The lucifer flame continued to burn down. Only seconds left now.

I quickly shifted the paper and foliage and in shifting them, saw the trouble. The leaves wouldn't burn. Even though they looked dead, there must be traces of life shot through them, stubbornly resisting death.

I had only moments left.

I yanked the leaves from the fire material and set the last of the flame to the remaining stuff.

It worked. The flame took. The fire burned.

But this created another problem. The guard might not notice the fire right away. I'd hoped the leaves would slow the path of the burning. The material that was left would burn all too quickly. What if the guard didn't see it before it burned out?

I pushed the fire very near the entrance so that a blind man could probably spot it from where the guard stood. He might see me doing it, come up here, and we'd have a shoot-out, me with my six-gun and him with his shotgun. But I didn't have any choice. I'd run out of tricks.

The fire burned. I crouched in the shadows on the right side of the entrance.

The way I knew he was coming was the jingling of his spurs. Somebody should have told this man that spurs weren't a good idea if you might conceivably need to move about invisibly. Spurs could get you killed.

I tried to be in his mind. He was responding to a fire. How did a fire ever get started in an empty gazebo?

He'd be hitching that shotgun up a little higher now. And his finger would be nervous on the trigger. And he'd be wondering if he maybe should have called out for help. But he'd seen the little fire and his instincts had taken over. And he was the self-reliant sort, so why should he call out for help when it was just this teeny-tiny fire and wouldn't he look like seven kinds of dipshit for calling out for help? They'd probably make fun of him — you know how the bunkhouse crowd was — they'd be on him for days.

But now that he was drawing closer —

Now that he was seeing this little fire —

This little fire that looked for all the world like it had been purposely set —

Well, he clutched his shotgun tighter, ready to shoot whenever he felt it was necessary —

That's what I would've been thinking anyway.

Then the jingling of his spurs got louder, closer by.

And that was when I got my first glimpse of his hat. It looked like a modified sombrero of some sort. And told you a lot about its owner. He'd be a jaunty cuss, this one, very dramatic in how he presented himself. Given to a lot of saloon self-mythologizing. Hell, I remember this one time down in Juarez, it was just me'n Bobby Lee Grunewald against these fourteen vaqueros, see? We didn't think we had a chance. But me'n Bobby Lee Grunewald, we jes' started a-shootin', and before you know it they was all dead, fourteen vaqueros layin' at our feet.

That sort of guy.

The one thing I'd need from him was his hat. That would get me into the mansion. Folks'd recognize the hat and let me pass.

He started up the entrance steps. The rowels of his spurs sounded like wind chimes.

I crouched down as low as I could get, ready to spring. Any moment now he'd be within range.

It looked as if he was going to cooperate because the first thing he did when he reached the inside of the gazebo was turn to look in the opposite direction at the fire that was flaming on the far side of the structure.

But then — maybe I made a noise; I was a little too big to be stealthy — he turned suddenly in my direction. And there I was. And he saw that there I was. And he swung that shotgun of his around so fast my stomach clenched even when I was in midair, flying toward him.

I'd rarely hit a man the way I hit him. Six, seven times full on in the face. Breaking the nose. Breaking several teeth. Bursting the lips. Then starting to pound on the forehead. The way he fell, backward without any hesitation at all, his head slamming against the floor next to the fire — I wondered if he was dead.

I relieved him of his shotgun, six-shooter, and sombrero. I took off his fancy kerchief and made a gag of it. Then I took off his belt and tied his arms together. My belt, I used on his ankles. I checked his pulse. Pretty strong. Which meant that he'd be awake sooner than later and come looking for me and warning the others. He wouldn't have too hard a time slipping his bonds. Belt knots don't last all that long.

Which meant I had to hurry.

I stamped out the fire, waved the smoke away into the night, where it flew like eerie gray bats toward the moonlight.

Hefting the shotgun, I left the gazebo

and slowly walked across the wide empty stretch of buffalo grass. The sombrero announced not only my presence but my identity. No reason to hurry, to draw any more attention to myself. I had to pretend I was the guard and act accordingly. He wouldn't have had a reason to run. And so I didn't either. I just took my time.

Till I reached the back door of the mansion.

No need for my skeleton keys. The door was open. I stepped inside. I was on a shadowy landing. Four steps up there was a door. A faint light bloomed in the line between door bottom and floor. I went up the steps on tiptoes. I was pretty sure, from the pleasant smells, that I was about to step into the kitchen.

I'd been in houses smaller than this kitchen. Truly. Webley was famous for his dinners and parties. It probably took a place this large — huge cupboards on all four walls; double sinks; four iceboxes; pantries the size of living rooms in three of the walls; and a linoleum floor that sparkled like ice on a frosty morning. The smells of veal and wine and fresh hot bread lingered on the air, tonight's dinner no doubt.

I moved on tiptoes again.

A hallway. A grandfather's clock intoning

the time in a great doomful voice. Sconces ahead revealing a vast vestibule and the edge of a vast, upsweeping staircase. Doors on either side of me, most of them open a crack, giving me glimpses of a den, a music room, what appeared to be a gallerylike display of artwork, and a very male business office.

Footsteps descending the staircase.

An honest-to-God butler — right out of an English magazine — in dark business suit and high white collar carried a silver tray with a lone empty glass on it. I hid in the shadows of the staircase. He was too caught up in his own ceremonious air to even look around.

But even though he hadn't seen me, my heart was going at an oppressive rate. I'd spent a good deal of my life as a lawman without any particular fears. But the past twenty-four hours were making up for that.

I edged toward the vestibule, listening intently.

I heard no human sounds on this first floor. The butler had likely gone to the kitchen I'd just left.

I remained in place, only angling my head toward the staircase. After a minute or so, sounds began to drift down the steps, all the way to the chandelier, which was as big as the sun and probably twice as bright when it was lighted.

Human voices. Muffled.

Up the stairs was where I needed to go. And that would be even riskier than setting the fire in the gazebo.

But there wasn't much choice. No choice really.

I needed to find her, confront her. Then throw her in Webley's face and make him see the truth he'd been trying to deny or change.

His wife was the killer. And she would have to pay.

I started toward the stairs just as I heard soft footsteps coming toward me. The butler again. I barely had time to jerk back into the gloom on the side of the stairway.

He went upstairs, bearing his silver tray, a fresh drink in its center. He walked with perfect aggravating grace. Nobody should walk that way. Nobody should want to walk that way.

Then he was just a memory.

I decided to wait until he'd come back downstairs. The fewer people on the second floor, the safer I'd be.

It took him five very long minutes to re-appear and walk down the stairs. On the last step he paused to scratch his nose. I was glad he didn't pick it. It would have spoiled his dignity.

He turned right, back again to the kitchen.

I swung around the newel post and started taking the steps two tiptoes at a time. The mahogany gleamed in the moonlight through a skylight that had been cut into the roof.

Not a stair creaked as I climbed. But the nearer the top I got, the more I heard the sound of angry but muffled voices. Far down the hall to the right. I felt exposed, still in the silver rays of moonlight through the skylight.

I moved to the right, into the shadows occasionally cast back by small glass lamps along the walls.

I turned once to look back down the hall on the other side of the staircase. It looked pretty much like this side. Doors closed, small lamps along the wall, a sense of desertion because of all the empty space. This struck me as one of those huge houses that was more for show than for people to actually live in.

I worked my way down the hall and as I did so, the voices, not very loud even as I drew nearer, became vivid and recognizable. Laura and Paul. Arguing.

"I want to know what you did with her," Laura said.

"Byrum didn't have any right to tell you that."

"Well, he did tell me that, and now I want an answer."

"Well, he was lying."

She laughed harshly. "You actually think I'll believe that, Paul? That Byrum would just make up something like that?"

A silence. Then Paul: "I'm doing this for your sake."

"Oh, yes. I'm sure."

"You know the truth and I know the truth, and we have to deal with it."

"But you don't know the truth, Paul. You only think you do."

"Blood all over you —"

"But the blood was only —"

"That's the truth, Laura. That's the truth. And you know it and I know it. And I understand why you did it. But I've got to protect you for your own sake. If anybody ever finds out what happened back East —"

"That was ten years ago! And it was self-defense."

"That's not what your father says. Or believes. If he hadn't been able to get that judge to let you go to the asylum instead of prison —"

"The asylum was worse than prison, believe me."

"Nonetheless, Laura, if you'd been found guilty and gone to prison, your life would've been destroyed."

"And you've been reminding me of that ever since the day you met me. Ever since the day you and my father decided to send me to another prison — living with you."

He slapped her.

A cry followed. Not hers. His. Her words had probably hurt him far more than his slap had hurt her. She'd get over the slap. He'd never get over the words.

"I shouldn't have said that, Paul. I'm sorry."

"I'm sorry I slapped you. I never should've —"

"I know you're only trying to help me, Paul, but —"

"You didn't remember the other one either. You honestly didn't remember. When you stabbed the other one. The doctors had some kind of fancy word for it. But all I know is that you couldn't face what you'd done. And so you just blocked it from your mind. And that's what's happening here, Laura. You may not be able to see it. But I can. And I've got to protect you. That's all your father ever asked me to do. To protect you; to keep you safe from other people and — yourself."

"God." She laughed. But this was a soft laugh. "Being pretty is a curse. People think I'm making that up when I say it. But all my life men have treated me like a little doll they want to collect and put on the shelf and show off to their friends. Even my father was that way. Always wanting to show his men friends how pretty and delicate I was. And what I really was was a tomboy. That's what I was really like. I loved playing rough with my brothers. And building birdhouses in the woods. And jumping naked into the lake near our house. I hated all those piano recitals and little plays they used to make me put on. I always swore that when I got to be an adult —"

"Did Steve Reynolds let you be a tomboy?" Webley's voice was tight. He obviously held no fondness for this Steve Reynolds.

"Are you kidding? He was the worst of all. He wanted me for sex and to put me on display. Then he didn't even want me for sex anymore. He had several mistresses. I think he got bored with having a wife who was as boring as I was. And God, was I boring. I did just what he wanted me to

— I really did love him — and it turned out that we both hated what I'd turned myself into."

"And then you killed him."

"It was self-defense."

"Laura, listen. That was what your father's lawyers convinced the judge of. That it was self-defense. But you actually don't remember what happened. I'm convinced of that and so were your doctors. But if you're ever put on trial for killing Stanton —"

"I didn't kill Stanton —"

"If you're ever put on trial for killing Stanton, that old trial back East will be dredged up. And how will it look then?"

"I didn't kill him."

"All right, Laura. Let's say I believe that. But put yourself on the jury. You'll have to admit you were in his hotel room the night Stanton was murdered. You'll have to admit that you had blood on your clothes. You'll have to admit that you were very angry with him. You'll have to admit —"

She then uttered a word most women in these parts don't use very often. Then she said, "Poor Callie."

"It's either poor Callie or poor Laura. One of you will have to be blamed for killing Stanton. Are you willing to throw away your life?"

"How'll you ever get her to admit that she killed him, Paul?"

"I still haven't figured that out yet."

"You're not going to hurt her? You promise?" Laura said.

"I promise."

"I didn't kill him."

A rustle of garments. An embrace. "Promise me you won't hurt her, Paul."

Garments rustling again. Another embrace.

I was so caught up in listening — no theatrical had ever been half as fascinating — that I didn't hear him. I just felt the aggravating stab of his six-shooter in my back.

He had a very formal voice; it matched his demeanor very well.

"I believe Master Paul will be wanting to speak to you, sir."

"Since when do butlers carry guns?"

He said quite crisply, "I do what's necessary to protect the master, sir."

He stepped around me and knocked on the door behind which Laura and Paul were talking.

TWENTY-TWO

"Go away," Webley said from the other side of the door.

"It seems you have an uninvited guest, sir."

"What the hell are you talking about, Greaves?"

"The former town marshal, sir. He somehow got into the house and has been eavesdropping on the conversation between you and your wife."

The door seemed to implode. And in its frame, looking fierce as a gladiator, was Webley. I no longer saw him as an ineffectual little man who paid you back through subterfuge. Any man can be dangerous — hell, any woman, too — when they reach a certain level of rage. And he'd certainly reached that level.

He came at me swinging. I leaned to the side. His first punch missed. But not his second. He was smaller and not as fast, but he clipped me hard in the ribs and it hurt.

"This isn't going to do any good," I said.

"Maybe not for you."

He had to literally jump up to get me in the face, but jump up he did. His fist caught me on the side of the mouth and drew instant blood.

I held my temper. I cared only about one thing. Finding Callie. A fistfight wasn't going to help me do it.

Laura shouted, "Paul! This is stupid! You're making a fool of yourself!"

"This is my house and you don't belong here!"

Everybody feels that their own home is sacred. You probably feel a lot more like that when your home happens to be a mansion.

He came at me again, but this time I defended myself. He was an inch off the floor when I knocked him back into the den, a huge room with book-lined walls, an ornamental Victorian fireplace mantel, and a wall of awards and plaques all certifying that the man in this room with its heavy furnishings, vast standing globe, and walls of books and floor covered with genuine Persian rugs — was every bit as important as he thought he was.

I got him in a neck lock and flung him against his desk. I was on top of him before he could find his feet. I took him by the hair and threw him into a leather armchair.

"Stay there."

"You don't order me around in my house."

"Sure I do. I've got every right as a citizen to arrest you."

"The hell you have."

"I heard what your wife said, Webley. Where's Callie?"

I sounded a lot cooler than I felt. What I wanted to do was tear his face off. But that wouldn't get me Callie. Only patience and steady pressure would get me Callie. If she was still alive.

"Tell him," Laura said. Then to me: "I didn't have anything to do with this, Morgan."

She wore a form-fitting emerald-colored green dress that had a certain regal cut to it. The Queen would soon be receiving her in the grand ballroom, no doubt. I was sick of them both — sick of all the Webleys in the world, and sick of all their Lauras — all their power, all their cunning, all their selfishness. I had to hold myself back from working them over with my pistol.

"Where is she, Webley?"

"I didn't hurt her."

"I want to see that for myself."

"I imagine he'll let you, sir."

I'd forgotten the butler. He moved with a

kind of arthritic dignity, standing over his fallen master, who was sprawled in the leather chair. He handed Webley the six-shooter and said, "Byrum and Aikins are on the way from the bunkhouse. I signaled them."

"Thank you, Greaves."

At any other time, I would have been interested in their signaling system. But right now all I cared about was Callie.

"You're forcing my hand, Marshal," Webley said, composing himself in the chair, pointing his weapon directly at me.

"Yeah. And I'll bet you'll hate to kill me, too."

"I didn't ask you to come here tonight."

"No, you just kidnapped my wife."

"You love your wife, and I love my wife," he said reasonably enough. "You'd do just what I'm doing to save her. You know you would."

"If Laura's as dangerous as you say, this is going to happen again, Webley. And you know it. People like Laura — it goes on, Webley. It repeats and repeats and repeats. That's why they have to stay in sanitariums and asylums. You think you can change her, Webley. But you can't. She probably thinks she can change herself. But she can't do it either. She is what she is."

Laura, ever beautiful, ever delicate and dignified, stepped in front of me and said, "I hate to disappoint you, Morgan, but I'm sure I didn't kill Stanton."

"By saying you're sure you didn't — what you mean is you're *not* sure, Laura." I turned back to Webley. "I want my wife, Webley. Now."

He stood up and said, "Come in, men."

Neither Byrum nor Aikins were outsized in any way. But they had handled and handled well so many dangerous situations in their years as cowboys that they walked into the room with the quiet confidence only experience can give you.

Webley didn't need to speak to them. They'd no doubt been in situations like this before. All he did was nod to Byrum.

Byrum took his gun from his holster and stepped over to me. He pointed to the gun in my own holster. We didn't speak either. I handed it over.

Aikins was the one doing the dirty work. He stood at an angle to me. He used his Colt. He got me hard on the side of my skull. I can't tell you anything more about that particular moment except that patterns began forming in the darkness in front of my eyes. And then there was this pain that traversed the top of my skull and ran all the way down the left side of my head and neck and right into my shoulder. And then I was falling. Somebody said something. But I had no idea what it was. And that was just about it except that, vaguely, I felt worse when my head slammed against the floor. Not even the expensive Persian rug could buffer the pain.

TWENTY-THREE

Cold. Dark. Bumpy.

Pain from full bladder. Pain from lying wrong on my right shoulder. Pain from being struck by Aikins and then my head trying to split the hardwood floor apart.

Cold. Dark. Bumpy.

Jingle of traces. Squeak of wagon wheels. Snort of horses.

I was in the bed of a buckboard. My wrists and ankles were bound tight with rawhide strips. I was gagged.

The moon and the stars looked chill and autumnlike for such a warm night. I couldn't smell fall coming. But I could see it in the somber moods. There were Indian tribes that believed they could tell the seasons by noticing the subtle variations in the surface of the moon. I had a pretty good idea of the message it was sending me.

I leaned up, fighting my bonds, to see who was on the wagon seat. Aikins and Webley. Aikins driving.

We were heading north, into the territory where the last serious gold strikes had gone bust about ten years earlier. All that was left was an enormous boot hill and a ghost town filled with empty buildings that criminals hid out in sometimes. The only other residents were rats and stray dogs and the occasional coyote.

A good place to keep a prisoner, a ghost town. Leave a couple of guards with her, nobody would bother her. Keep her bound and gagged the way I was, she wouldn't even have a chance of screaming for help.

Poor Callie. I knew about where she was now. And I could also figure out what they wanted her to do. And as soon as she did it — Well, there were two of us to kill now. Ordinarily, Webley probably wouldn't have had the will for something like this. But as he'd said, when your wife's life was at stake —

The buckboard jounced and bounced and bumped and thumped. Aikins and Webley talked every once in a while, but in voices so low it was as if they were afraid they might awaken me or something.

We were heading into a draw, the mountain slopes steep and ragged on either side. Streamlike music played its cool clear song. Usually such natural sights would have pleased me. But all I could think

about was Callie. I didn't necessarily believe Webley's word that she was still alive.

I began to recognize the place as soon as
the buckboard reached the rutted main
street. The ghost town of Harbor. It had
had two booms — one sparked by placer
gold and another, following the tapping
out of that placer gold, in quartz mining.
The problem being that quartz mining was
wasteful and expensive. So that boom, too,
tapped out. It always amazed me how
quickly boomtowns became ghost towns.
Harbor went from a prostitute-filled,
three-hotel gambling den of nearly eight
thousand to what it was now — a grave-
yard of deserted and dying false fronts and
the remnants of the quartz work.

As we passed down the street, I gazed up
at the dark dead eyes of the hotel rooms.
Lively parties had been held in all of them,
no doubt. Now they looked out upon
decay and destruction.

The buckboard clattered to a stop.

Aikins jumped down, came around, and
dragged me out of the wagon bed. I could
take mincing little steps, my ankles bound
the way they were. He poked the barrel of
a shotgun into my back and pushed me up
the steps of a two-story building fronted by
a fading sign that said REGAL HOTEL.

There was nothing regal about it, at least not these days.

Inside, Aikins grabbed a lantern, got it going. Rich yellow light repelled shadow and let me see what a hotel looked like after dogs, cats, rats, coyotes, and maybe even a puma or two had had their way with it for many long years. The floor was covered with fecal droppings of many kinds. The little furniture that was left was similarly covered. The cushion backing of a once-fancy love seat had been clawed, stuffing like innards spilling out. The place was pretty damned chilly. It smelled of rotting wood and basement mildew.

Webley came in then. He nodded to Aikins, and Aikins pushed me toward the stairs. Going up them seemed to take forever. My bound wrists clung to the banister for purchase.

Aikins pushed me down the second-floor hall, stepped ahead of me, kicked a door open, and there we were. A chunky Mexican with a sawed-off shotgun sat in a chair, guarding her.

She didn't even wake up when Aikins stomped the door in. In the lantern light, I could see what they'd done to her. The broken nose. The black eyes. The busted lip.

As if sensing what I was feeling, Webley

said, "We only did what was necessary." He sounded apologetic. But no apology in the world could explain or forgive what I was seeing. Only the frail rise and fall of her chest told me that she was able to draw breath.

There was nothing I could do about it now. But later. Later, Webley would be the one lucky to draw breath.

Callie slept with three quilts over her. She wore a man's flannel shirt and at the top of it I could see a line of long underwear. The days would be hot in here, no doubt. But nights would be cold.

"I gave her something to help her sleep," Webley said as Aikins helped sit me down in a corner. "She'll be fine. For now. But if you love her, Marshal, you'd better convince her to do what I say. I want her to write a letter confessing she killed Stanton. She can say it was in self-defense. She can say that he fell on the knife when they were wrestling over it. I really don't care how she does it. As long as she does it."

He nodded to Aikins. That silent language again. The nod must have been eloquent and articulate in a way an outsider couldn't understand.

Aikins came over and relieved me of my gag.

"Help me, Marshal. Save your wife any more pain."

"You know I'm going to kill you, don't you?"

"I'm sure you'd like to. And I'm sure you'd try — under normal circumstances. But these aren't normal, Marshal. For one thing, you're tied up. For another, you'd have to deal with Aikins here. And as tough as you are, you aren't anywhere near as tough as he is. Or as young."

Aikins listened to all this without showing any expression on his broad, flat, prairie face.

"She should wake up in another couple of hours," Webley said. "Then I want you to talk to her. Tell her to do the sensible thing."

"And when she signs, then you kill us."

"Maybe not. I'll have the letter I need."

"And I'll have a bruised wife I can show to people. I'll tell them all about the conditions she wrote the letter under. And I'll mention who beat her into writing the letter."

"But you'll have to prove it, Marshal. A court of law locally — I think most folks would take my word over yours. I don't mean to pull rank, but I think I have a little more authority than you do in this area."

"You going to tell me about your great grandpappy now?"

That one angered him. "Never talk about my father in that tone. You understand, Marshal?"

I shrugged. "So, meanwhile, your wife goes free. What happens when she kills somebody next time?"

"There won't be any next time. I'm going to keep a very tight hold on her. Very tight."

"She'll get a chance. Unless you chain her in a basement somewhere."

"That's for me to worry about, Marshal. Right now, the only thing you should worry about is your wife here. We're going to hang on here until she wakes up and until you convince her to write that letter." Another nod to Aikins. "We're going to go fix some coffee. There's a working stove out there, believe it or not."

Aikins disappeared into the gloom beyond the door.

"I really don't want her to be beaten again, Marshal," Webley said from the doorway. "I don't much have the stomach for this sort of thing."

"I'm going to kill you, Webley."

He smiled briefly and then looked troubled. "Yes, I think you mentioned that once. And you know what? I don't blame you at all. I'd do the same thing if I were you actually. I really would." The hell of it was, I believed him.

Webley took the lantern. I sat in the room with my wife. She snored softly, turned on her side. A night bird's cry. Wind under the eaves. My straining against my bonds.

After a time, Webley and Aikins and the Mexican guard started talking. I couldn't make out the words. They'd be back soon enough. Maybe an hour. I tried to imagine what it would be like to see Callie beaten. And me unable to do anything about it.

The night bird again and again and again. He was as agitated as I was. He sounded angry and scared. As I was.

I was in a race. I had to get out of my bonds before they came back. There was no way I could let them beat Callie. I didn't even think about them killing us. Beating her would be enough.

It took me ten minutes to see that Webley and his men had forgotten the same thing I had: my spurs. If I could stretch —

I did stretch. My arms felt as if they were being ripped from their sockets as I tried over and over to touch my wrists to my spurs, which were reasonably sharp. Sharp enough to start rope unraveling anyway.

I was just starting to get somewhere — feeling the rowels bite into the rope — when Webley came in. He didn't say anything to me. He just walked over to the bed and there in the shadows pinched Callie on the cheek. He wanted to see if she was faking sleep. She didn't wake up, didn't even groan.

He walked back out. I could see just enough of his face to see that he was unhappy.

I went back to work, angling the metal teeth of my spurs into the rope, starting to tear its fiber.

Another five minutes and Webley was back. "I thought I heard voices."

"Not unless I was talking to myself." I'd managed to pull myself upright again, so that he'd have no hint that I was stretching to reach my spur.

He came over to me, looked me up and down. He was smart enough to assume that I'd try to escape, but not smart enough to figure out the way I'd do it. He walked out silently again.

I worked harder, faster this time. The rope came apart in tangled sections. Even where thin strands were all that held it together, pulling it apart was difficult. Strong rope. Stronger than this particular lawman anyway.

And then it snapped.

My back was to the doorway. I enjoyed idiotic glee for a full minute — my hands apart, rope dangling from each wrist — before I heard the trigger being pulled back on a six-shooter.

"You put on quite a show," Aikins said. "Webley figured out what you were doin' the first time he came in here. We bet a couple of dollars you couldn't do it in under twenty minutes. I bet on you."

"You're good at that," Webley said, walking down the short hall to this room. "I didn't think you could do it at all, let alone under twenty minutes. Here's your money, Aikins."

Just then, Callie stirred. I had a sense she was going to sit up in bed, all wide awake and glad to see me. But soon enough, her breathing returned to its dull, flat repetition and she didn't move at all.

"Tie him up, Aikins."

Aikins tied me up. And soon after that, they left the room. The night bird again. My friend. The only creature in the world who understood how I felt at this moment. The frustration. The rage. The shame at being so helpless. The way Aikins had doubled his knots and wound the rope twice round, I wouldn't be doing any circus tricks this time. Oh, no, not this time.

She was ghost-white and frail in the moonbeam that splintered on a piece of timber stretching across a hole in the roof. And when she started to raise her head, I had a terrible vision of her stirring in her coffin, what she'd look like in such a circumstance. A good number of people were being buried alive these days, a problem even the government was lately addressing with federal regulations for burials.

She said nothing at first, her torso following her neck and head so that she sat straight up now. Her eyes revealed nothing, though I had the sense that she thought she was in some kind of dream. After what she'd been through, all of this was probably unreal. She would have looked more ethereal if she'd been dressed in a flowing white nightgown. But her clothes were coarse and homely, the flannel shirt and a couple of layers of underwear. Sleep drugs often gave people chills.

She didn't seem to see me. She sat there rigid, looking around, but somehow her eyes never finding mine. She was still probably wondering if she was in a trance of some kind.

And then, abruptly, as if I'd said something, she turned her head and saw me. She said, "Oh, my God, Lane, is that really you?"

Since the gag was back in my mouth — and I'd been a bad boy and Webley wanted to punish me so that I'd remember what happened to bad boys — all I could do was mutter against the gag.

Recognition came to her then. Her eyes narrowed. Her face seem to draw tight with purpose. She slipped out of bed.

It was obvious that she not only knew who I was, but knew what the situation was. She knew enough not to talk or make any noise.

She hitched up the denims she wore with her belt and then crossed over to me, taking long enough to kiss me tenderly on the cheek before she set to work on the ropes on my wrists. She used her fingernails and her teeth. Aikins had done a damned good job.

She stopped once — fear showing on her sweet face — when she heard somebody starting to walk back here. Then they paused and retreated.

She worked all the faster. First the wrist bonds. Then, working with me, the ankle bonds.

The footsteps again. I pointed to the bed. She nodded and hurried to it, resumed the position she'd been in when Webley was here last time.

After taking my left boot off, I waited flat against the wall on the west side of the door.

The footsteps coming closer.

I don't believe I've ever hit a man with such fury. I wasn't even sure who it was at first. I just let the person get two steps across the threshold and then I put all my anger into the punch into the back of his skull.

The Mexican was unconscious immediately. To make sure he stayed that way, I pounded him with the heel of my boot, the rowels of the spur opening up a bloody trench across the neck just above the rear collar of his shirt.

I got his Colt and I got his sawed-off. We were pretty well set.

"Hey, Juarez, you all right back there?" Aikins shouted.

Frozen silence.

"Juarez? You hear me?"

"You better go back and check on him," Webley said.

"Damned Mex," Aikins said. "I told you not to hire him."

"His father worked for my father. He comes from a very nice family." That was the thing about Webley. He was the original good-bad man.

Callie started to get out of bed. I waved her back. I didn't want her near the line of fire.

Aikins started walking back to us. In the silence I could hear him cock his gun. Violence came easily to a man like Aikins. He wasn't a mad dog. He was simply a professional.

He paused just before Callie's room. I could imagine the calculations he was making at this moment. Moonlit room. Callie in bed, apparently still sleeping. And me — That was what shook him. I was nowhere to be seen.

"Better bring your shotgun with you, Mr. Webley," he called out. "The marshal's playing games with us."

I had maybe a minute before Webley would be standing next to Aikins. I knew what I had to do. Would I be fast enough?

I took three steps out into the frame of the door and said, "Drop your gun, Aikins."

He fired twice and so did I. I had the advantage in that I'd been in the dark a lot longer than he'd been. My eyes had adjusted to it. He had to contend with his vision and with me throwing myself back out of the door frame after squeezing off my two shots. I'd hit him twice somewhere between the belt line and the throat. I had no clearer idea than that. He made a lot of noise hitting the floor.

And then he was crying the way men do when they know they're dying. We don't know how to cry very well under the best of circumstances, and with death it's the same. He seemed embarrassed to be crying, choking it off every quarter minute or so. It took a minute for my eyes to find the exact spots where he'd been hit. Just to the right of his heart. Just under the thyroid.

"I wish I could see my mama," he said.

I know how that sounds. A gunny saying something like that. But we won't be any different than that, you or me. Heroic dying's for the dime novelists. When real people die real deaths, we tend to sound like five-year-olds and our minds are filled with images of yesterdays when we were little and our moms and dads were there to protect us.

But there was no protecting Aikins. Not now. He went into some kind of jig there on the floor, kicking out so hard that his spurs ripped the wooden floor. He was muttering names and places I'd never heard of before. It was sad, and I took no pleasure in watching it. He'd no doubt taken a turn at beating Callie. But there's one thing about revenge — most of us don't like to see ourselves as madmen. And that's what revenge usually turns us into. A lot of times we become worse than the man we're trying to repay in kind.

Then he was back on this plane of existence: "Shoot me, Marshal. I'm a dead man anyway. I can't take this pain."

"You sure?"

Blood seeped thick and dark from the corner of his mouth. "I'm sure."

"You want to say a prayer or something?"

"You know a prayer you could say for me? I'd appreciate it."

"It's a Catholic prayer."

He startled me by smiling. "Right now I don't reckon I care what kind of prayer it is. I never had much truck with you fish-eaters. But I guess this'll have to do me, won't it?"

I said a prayer from the funeral mass, asking the Lord to take Aikins to his side.

He didn't make it through the prayer. Not quite. Life left him. He became a statue that had been defaced with blood.

His bowels had run down his legs and the smell was pretty bad.

Webley, near the front of the place, made a noise. Then stopped. Behind me, Callie started to get out of bed. I waved her off again.

I said, "Webley, I said I'd kill you. But I'll tell you what. You come back here and lay down your guns, I'll take you back to town."

"And then you'll get Laura arrested."

"She killed Stanton."

"She's my wife — and she's not right in the head. It's not her fault."

"That'll be for somebody else to decide. I killed Aikins and I'll kill you if I need to."

"I won't let her be put in prison."

"It's up to you, Webley. Put down your guns or I'll kill you. And I think you know me well enough to know that that's exactly what I'll do."

"He'll do it, Webley," said Callie. "I don't want to see you die. Please just give Morgan your guns."

"After all he did to you, you don't want to see him die?" I said quietly.

Callie shook her head. "You don't know how much he loves her, Morgan. He's crazy with it."

"What's your decision, Webley?" I barked.

A sob. Or something very much like it. A curse. And then the sob again. He said, "I'm walking back there, Morgan. Don't shoot."

It wasn't dramatic at all, if that's how you picture it. He just came back looking weary and sad. He walked right up to me — not paying any attention to the sawed-off I had leveled right at his belly — and started handing me guns. He had three of them. Two handguns and a shotgun. I dumped them on the end of the bed.

He looked at Callie. "I'm sorry, Callie. I'm really very sorry." And then he began to cry.

But I didn't give a damn about him crying. I set down the sawed-off and started in on him. I pounded his head and face, and then I pounded his belly and ribs, and then I went back to his head. He bled a lot and he screamed a lot. So did Callie, for that matter. Trying to stop me. But I couldn't be stopped. Not right then. I was into the simple animal rhythm and pleasure of it. Right now I didn't give a damn that I was turning into the same sort of bully Webley had been to Callie.

I cut him enough that he bled a lot; and I inflicted enough pain that he begged me to stop. And I would've kept right on going, but Callie was dragging me off him, hitting me with her fists, even kicking me a few times in the leg. "Can't you see he's hurt? Can't you see what you're doing to him?"

When the average person gets violent, he often tells you how he acted in a hazy, dreamlike state. Like it was somebody else beating his opponent, or stabbing him or shooting him. The whole thing wasn't — and would never be — quite real.

And that was how I felt when all of Callie's slaps, punches, and kicks collected enough power to bring me back from whatever stay of frenzy and rage I'd allowed myself to slip into.

At my feet — this was in the all-too-real world — lay a bloody heap named Webley. The heap was sobbing and gasping and moaning.

And then Callie was running to find water and rags — maybe the same water and rags they'd used on her — and then rushed back to minister to him. The same man who'd kidnapped her. The same man who'd beaten her. The same man who would've ordered her death as soon as she'd signed the false confession.

She got him up on the bed and got his shirt off, and looked him over with the careful eye a doc would apply.

"Nothing broken," she told him.

"My nose."

"Bruised, not broken."

"I had it coming."

"Lord," she said. "You men and your anger. It makes me sick."

She continued to take care of him. She sent me out front to find some whiskey. When she took control like this, there was no sense arguing. You did what she told you to, or there would be hell to pay.

But I couldn't quite let it go. "Even after all he did to you you're defending him?"

"I'm not defending him, Morgan. I'm trying to make you understand him is all. That's the difference." She pointed to him. "Now help me get him outside and on his horse."

The Mexican grunted and stirred slightly.

"Get him some water, Morgan."

I laughed. "Remind me not to invite you to a hanging. You'll let the prisoner go."

But I got him some water. He sat Indian-legged and drank it. And then daubed some on the wound from where I'd hit him. "You hit hard."

"So do you, I imagine. But I didn't want to find out."

"Bad headache, man."

I nodded to Aikins. "Could've been worse."

"He put up a fight, eh?"

"He tried," I said.

I stuck a hand out. Helped pull him to his feet. The Mexican was winded. He kept staring at Aikins. "Next week was his birthday. His daughter's coming here from New Mexico to see him."

"I'm sorry."

He smiled. "No, you're not. You're a lawman. Lawmen don't give a shit about people they kill."

"Sounds like you've made your mind up already. Guess there's no reason to try and change it."

He went hard-ass on me. Glaring. His mouth a sneer. "Lawmen killed my little brother, man. You ain't no different than them." He dug a toothpick from his shirt pocket, jammed it in his teeth, and walked out of the deserted hotel ahead of me.

I grabbed one side of Webley, Callie the other. We got him out to his horse. His face looked puffy and bloody in the stark moonlight.

The Mexican smirked at me. "You do good work, man. Mr. Webley, he lucky he be alive."

"Leave him alone," Webley said.

The Mexican shrugged. "It's your face, Boss. Personally, I'd want a crack at him sometime. Pay him back."

Webley looked at me and laughed through an obviously sore mouth. "You ask Morgan's wife how see feels about paying people back."

"I ain't afraid of no woman," the Mexican said.

"This one you should be," Callie said, coming out of the hotel. She'd gone back in to get the prayer book she'd brought with her.

The Mexican looked at her, said nothing.

I helped Callie up on her horse. She was set. Then I swung up on my horse. We had a good long ride ahead of us.

I was going to bring Laura Webley in and all this nonsense was finally going to be over.

I checked on Webley. He looked as if he was about ready to pitch out of the saddle. I said, "You going to be all right?"

"That's kind've a funny question coming from you, isn't it, Marshal?"

We set off for the mansion.

TWENTY-FOUR

The place was dark when we arrived. No-body was home in the magic castle. Probably even the alligators in the moat were sleeping.

From about a quarter mile away, Webley started saying, like a nervous aunt, over and over, "Something's wrong. There should be some lights on."

He was right. It was odd. Why would the huge Victorian house be so dark?

As we drew nearer in the shadows, I saw a faint light on the second floor, near the west side of the mansion.

"They're probably sleeping," I said. "It's late."

"She was very upset when I left," Webley said. "She could never fall asleep when she was that upset. She can barely sleep even with all those stupid potions the doctor gives her. They just make her groggy half the time."

As we reined in, I glanced at Callie. I think we both had the same sense. That something terrible had happened here. Hard to know what it was exactly. But I was sure we'd soon find out.

Webley was still wobbly. I was starting to regret the beating I'd given him. Not so much because of him but because of me. I didn't like to lose control like that. I'd spent most of my life as a professional lawman. One of the things that meant was staying sane and sober while all about you people were frothing with rage.

I didn't like to think of myself as giving into the same crazy impulses.

Webley moved faster than I thought he could have. We went in the back door. He lighted a lamp in the kitchen and led us through the house. Even under these conditions — the feeling that something bad was in the air — it was hard not to stare at all the antiques and pieces of art he'd accumulated. Or rather, that Laura had accumulated.

He started shouting her name. His voice quickly rose to a level of hysteria. Shouting her name and bumping wildly into furniture, he moved from room to room.

We were headed to the vestibule and the staircase. And that light I'd spotted on the second floor.

He alternated now. Shouting her name and then the butler's; her name and then the butler's.

By the time we reached the bottom of

the staircase, the butler appeared at the top of it and said, "Marshal, I think you'd best keep the master down there."

"What the hell are you talking about?" Webley screamed.

The butler's words had only made him more hysterical. They'd been meant to calm, I suppose. But I had to say they would have had the same effect on me. They were ominous and terrible words.

Webley took the stairs two at a time. When he reached the top, the butler tried to grab him, but Webley shoved him away. Then he disappeared down the hall.

Callie and I were halfway up the stairs when Webley cried out. I don't think I've ever heard anything like that. A kind of strangling grief. Sad and not a little bit insane.

The butler turned left and ran down the second-floor hall. We moved faster up the steps.

Webley wasn't hard to find. He was shrieking and smashing everything in the room he was in. A windowpane broke; a heavy piece of something slammed into the wall. And now he started sobbing.

I thought of the asylum Laura had spent so much time in. Webley himself seemed like a good candidate for one at this point.

The butler stood outside the door. He

stepped back into the shadows when we reached him.

We went inside and saw her. Or what was left of her anyway.

She'd put the Colt in her mouth. That was the only way to do it if you wanted to be absolutely safe. I've seen them put it to their forehead and their temple and still not die. But I've never seen them put it in their mouth and not die. You don't get any reprieve with that method.

By this time, Webley had sunk into a chair and had his face in his hands. He was no longer sobbing. It was as if by covering his eyes, he could will us — and his dead wife — out of his mind.

I checked her the way I would have any other corpse. I tried for pulse points. I tried to find the wound up in her mouth. I tried to cover as much of the mess as I could by taking the pillowcase off, spreading it over the wormy remnants of her brain splattered all over the bed. This was apparently the guest room. Twin beds, a small bookcase, even a small bar. It all resembled a very nice hotel room.

The letter had fallen off the other side of the bed. Apparently, in his blinding grief, Webley hadn't seen it.

I picked it up.

Dear Paul,

You were far truer to me than I ever was to you. I was never a good wife or, even, a good friend. I was so bored with my life here that when I met David Stanton, I was ready to throw everything away. I risked it all. I knew what he was, of course, and I didn't care. I just wanted some escape from my deadly dull routine. I'm very sorry I was so foolish. I owed you my loyalty, if nothing else. You were very, very good to me, Paul. And right now — in this last moment of my life — I recognize just how good and I really appreciate it. I must've gone into the same kind of blackout I did back East, when that murder took place. I don't remember killing Stanton, but I realize now that I must have. That's why I went to see him. To kill him. He was going to run out on me. He'd promised he'd take me with him. But he always lied. Always. I'm so sorry for how I ruined our lives, Paul. Now please find yourself another woman — a good, sensible, sane one this time.

Love,
Laura

I didn't think Webley was ready for it yet, so I folded it in half and stuck it in my shirt pocket. I went back over to Callie.

"The poor woman," she said.

"Yeah," I said, "she was."

Webley chose then to take his hands down from his face. "There's bourbon on that bar over there. Would somebody get me a drink?"

I didn't like being ordered about by rich men, but I decided this was a special circumstance. I got him a hefty drink of bourbon. Took him the glass.

"I saw the letter," he said.

"I'll have to turn it over to the law."

"I keep forgetting you're not the law."

"That'd be Tom Ryan from now on."

"I hate to ask you this — you mind taking Callie into town and clearing all this up? You can take the letter. I just don't feel much like talking."

I slid my arm around Callie's waist. "She's going home to bed. I'll take this letter into town and talk to Tom about it. But I expect you to turn yourself in by tomorrow noon."

I was surprised that he was surprised. "Turn myself in? Isn't this —" He nodded to the dead woman on the bed. "Isn't this enough?"

"No," I said, "it's not. You kidnapped a woman and held her captive. You also beat her. You've got some serious trouble, Webley. And this time your influence isn't enough to get you out of it."

He put his face in his hands again. Left them there for some time. I glanced at Callie. Thank God she wasn't going sympathetic about him now. Anybody else would have to stand trial; so should he.

"I'll hunt up your lawyer and tell him what happened," I said to Webley. "I'll have him meet you at his office at ten o'clock."

"I just can't believe that you're going to charge me."

"You couldn't believe that I was going to charge your son either. You might've forgotten, but that's what started this whole thing. That trouble Trent got into. You should've just let it ride out its course. Look where the hell it led, Webley. You can't be too happy about that."

When we left, Webley sat on the edge of the bed, touching a tentative hand to his wife's face. The dead eyes expressed a certain surprise. I suppose that first moment of the death sensation is a surprise. Whatever you think it's going to be, it's probably different.

The butler saw us out. At the back door, he said, "He's never going to be the same."

"Good," I said. "He needed to change."

As we walked down the sloping hill to our horses, Callie said, "You're getting to be so cold, Morgan. We all need to change. None of us is perfect."

"It's this town," I said. "I need to get far away and fast."

She slid her arm through mine. "I assume you're planning to take me with you."

"I'll think it over and let you know."

She unslid her arm and used her fist to punch me in the kidney. "Think it over and let me know. And right now."

"All right, I'll take you with me. Just don't hit me anymore."

The moon was full and high and solemn as we rode home. Callie seemed to grow stronger the closer we got. She said, "I'm rid of him finally."

"We all are."

She didn't have to tell me it was Stanton we were talking about.

"I wonder if she really killed him."

"If she didn't," I said, "why would she have written that letter?"

"Because she wasn't well. Because she was always imagining things that hadn't really happened. Because maybe if Webley kept telling her she'd killed him, maybe she started to believe it herself."

I laughed. "I thought you wanted this to be over."

"I do."

"Then let's leave it alone. Laura Webley killed Stanton. We have her confession. And her husband agrees that she did it."

"Don't you see what could've happened?" Callie said as we drew close to our place, all limned with silver in the moonlight.

"No, I guess I don't."

"Webley knew how suggestible Laura was. What if he killed Stanton and then convinced her she did it?"

"Webley has an alibi. The butler said he was at home that night."

"You don't think the butler would lie for him?"

As we dismounted, I said, "You're hard, you know that? You're little and pretty and delicate. But you're hard. You get something in your mind and it stays there, and then you fight for it like a snake I just stepped on."

"I've always wanted to be compared to a snake."

I got all sentimental and carried her across the threshold. I set her down on the bed and said, "I'd better not sit down with you."

"Why not?"

"Because then I might get certain kinds of ideas."

"I wouldn't let you anyway," she said. "I need a bath and a good night's sleep before I'd even think about that." She took my hand, touched it to her cheek. "Ouch." She'd rubbed my hand against one of her many facial bruises. Not to mention her nose. "But you think about what I said, Morgan, all right? He could've killed Stanton and then made Laura think she did it."

"Maybe," I said. "But probably not. Laura seemed pretty convinced she'd killed him."

Callie put on a pot of coffee, drew back the covers, and said, "I guess I'll just clean up at the sink tonight. You think you could stand sleeping next to me?"

"I might just survive."

"You're sure in good spirits."

I took her in my arms. To hell with her washing. "Why shouldn't I be? I've got my wife back, and I'm in the clear as far as my job goes."

"Won't that be hard on Ryan?"

"I'll try and get him a raise. I think I can swing him a pretty good one. The town council'll want to be nice to me for a while. For not trusting me. I'll have some leverage so I can help Tom."

"They should, and just for the way he had to wrestle that Conroy — that con artist — on the stage the afternoon Stanton was killed. He really didn't want to go. He said he had a right to be here."

I laughed. "Con artists are getting bolder these days. They think you shouldn't be able to do anything to them — like run them out of town — when they start cheating people."

Just before she let her clothes fall away, she said, "How about turning down the lantern?"

"At least you didn't ask me to go outside this time."

"I just never got used to being nude around you. You should be happy I've got a little modesty left. A girl like me with a past like mine."

"Yeah, you and Belle Star."

"Well, I'm not exactly an angel."

"You come pretty close."

"You're stalling, lawman. Turn down the lamp."

Which I did. But I didn't mention that sitting at the table and watching her moonbeam-traced silhouette was even more erotic than watching her lamp-lit. I don't suppose it was pure sex I wanted. I wanted the physical and mental reassurance that she was really back and free of suspicion. And free of Stanton.

As she began to dry herself off, I couldn't hold back any longer. I walked over to her and held her face to mine and kissed her in a gentle way that stirred both of us nonetheless. She decided to bathe me, too. Was I going to say no? Thus, a lot cleaner than we'd been, we slipped into bed and proceeded to make the sort of love that would make twenty-year-olds envious. The second time through, slower now, a little talk here and there now, she started to cry. She said it wasn't for any particular reason; that it was just an expiation of sorts. The way coming was an expiation sometimes — not simply heady pleasure but a cleansing, too, a rebirth.

And then we fell asleep in a position so awkward that one of us would have ordinarily untwisted ourself out of it. But not tonight. Awkward or not, we remained in that position until well after every rooster, dog, cat, bird, and horse in the valley was up and making its own particular kind of racket.

I had to get up and head to town. I let her sleep.

TWENTY-FIVE

By the time I reached the town marshal's office, the word about Laura Webley had apparently been spread around pretty well. Just about everybody I saw waved and grinned at me. Even a couple of old foes waved. They didn't like me but on the other hand, they probably hadn't wanted to believe I was a killer either.

Tom Ryan was holding his morning meeting with the deputies. I could hear his voice all the way up the hall from his office. He sounded pretty damned authoritative. I sure hadn't sounded that confident when I was his age. I poured myself a cup of coffee and sat down to wait up front.

At first I just couldn't believe what I was hearing. I recognized the voice before the words took on meaning. What would he be doing here?

But soon enough what he was doing here was clear. He said, "I got the town council out of bed early this morning and they've assured me that I'm right on this matter. They're going to back me completely. And

I told them that I'd talk to Tom here and that I was sure Tom's men would go along with it, too."

"But Morgan's a friend of ours," somebody said.

"He hired every one of us. Taught us everything we know."

"It's time for Morgan to move on," the voice of Webley said. Webley, the man I'd left grieving over the dead body of his wife, had recovered remarkably. And was plotting to get me out of town permanently so that neither his son Trent nor himself would be charged for anything. The fact that Tom Ryan hadn't spoken up in my behalf — Well, even the best friendships end. Tom had a family to feed. And he'd always wanted to be marshal.

I started thinking about what Callie had said and it started making sense. Given Laura's mental condition, it had probably been easy enough to convince her that she'd killed Stanton. Easy enough for her husband anyway. She'd written out the letter and killed herself. He probably hadn't even helped her with it. Given her unstable mind, she hadn't needed any help.

Webley had murdered Stanton and managed to have his wife die for what he'd done. I was his last obstacle in town. With his money and influence, he'd now run the town council and the marshal's office and be a happy man. Likely there'd be another young, delicate woman in his life in a seemly time. He'd want people to think that he was mourning Laura before he brought another rare flower home. And Trent wouldn't be doing even a day of jail time. Tom would drop the charges. And if the county attorney got fussy about it, well, county attorneys could be replaced just like town marshals.

I finished off my coffee and went outside. I leaned against the hitching post and rolled myself a cigarette.

The town made me lonesome. I'd gotten used to the slant of sunlight on the peaked roof of the Lutheran church; and the cry of pigeons echoing off the underside of the roof of the bandstand in the park; and watching the angle of horse necks as the shiny animals dipped their heads to drink from the trough.

I was lonesome for the way the town had been a few years ago when it seemed that there was a true desire to lessen the influence of both the Webleys and the Grices. But it had stalled somehow. Maybe I hadn't pushed hard enough. Or maybe I'd pushed too hard and spooked people away. Nobody could relish an open battle with Webley.

I heard the door open and them talking, the two of them, and then their boots on the boardwalk. They must have recognized me from my back because they suddenly stopped talking. They'd sounded so hearty just then, too, talking about the way things would be around here from now on.

I turned around and looked at them. That's all. Just looked. And that's all it took. Ryan froze. Embarrassed. His mouth opened but nothing came out.

Webley just shook his head. "If you came to town to cause trouble, Morgan, you're too late." He'd never looked smaller or more nervous. He'd bought himself a new town marshal and he was still afraid. It didn't say much for being the most powerful man in the valley.

"You should look a lot happier," I said to Webley. "You're back in control."

"How could I look happy? My wife just died."

"Maybe you wanted her to," I said.

"And just what the hell's that supposed to mean?" Then he put a halting hand up in the air. "No, don't tell me. I'm sick of your theories. My wife was a disturbed woman. She shot and killed the man she'd taken up with. I have to live with that the rest of my life. I'll be damned if I let you punish me any worse with your lies."

Gently, Ryan said, "Maybe you'd better go have yourself some coffee, Morgan."

"He buy you pretty cheap, did he?" I said to Ryan. The words came hard. We'd been good friends once. "He offered me five hundred dollars a month when I came to town. If I kept things favorable to him. You're a lot younger than I am, Ryan. You should be getting more money than that."

"Too bad you can't arrest a man for insolence, Ryan," Webley said.

Ryan still looked embarrassed.

There wasn't much point staying here. We could trade insults all morning, but that wouldn't change anything. Webley had his town back.

I glanced at them and then walked away. Ryan broke with Webley and hurried up to me. "I'm sorry about how things turned out."

The hell of it was, I supposed he really was sorry. We'd been friends. But he had a family and responsibilities, and he had to do what he needed to to survive.

"Be careful of him, Ryan. He looks like a mild little man. But he's as ruthless as his old man was. He just doesn't make as much noise about it." I took a few steps ahead, then stopped and glanced back at him. "There's a good chance Webley himself killed Stanton and then convinced his wife she did it."

I didn't wait for his reaction. I just walked over to the café, where I spent a good hour pouring coffee down myself and looking out the window at the town I'd soon be leaving. A number of people stopped by my table to say hello. I appreciated that. I'd have good memories of them and apparently they'd have good memories of me.

When I saw him come in the door, my hand automatically dropped to my gun. He was still the same, but not the same. The hair had been cut short, the beard stubble had been shaved off, the gunny duds had been exchanged for a plain blue cotton shirt and blue trousers. And the cockiness was nowhere to be found in the eyes or on the mouth. He saw me, too, and came straight over.

"I thought I put you on a stagecoach," I said.

"You did, Marshal," he said. "And that Ned Hastings kept right on going. He's probably got himself in a gunfight already. He may already be dead. I hope so because

I sure don't want to run into him again."

He sat down without being asked.

"I came back to town to apologize. And to thank you."

"For what?"

"For saving my life. I really thought I was a gunny. Then you put on that little demonstration in my hotel room and when I sobered up, I realized how much I'd been kidding myself. I could shoot the hell out of cans down by a crick. But as for an actual gunfight — So I came back here and cleaned myself up and got me a job over to the lumberyard. I start tomorrow morning."

You hear that people don't change. But they do. I've seen it dozens of time. Sometimes the changes don't last. But sometimes they do. Looked like the kid here was going to give it a real good try.

He said, "Ryan's the marshal now, huh?"

"Yeah."

"He seems like a decent enough sort."

"He is."

"I always felt sorry for him the nights we played cards."

"Cards?"

"Sure. At the hotel. The ones in Sanderson's room."

"He played cards there?"

"He did the two nights I did anyway."

His family. His debts. His trap. Why would he add to it by gambling? But the answer was easy enough. Desperate men do desperate things. He'd pay his way out of debt by gambling.

"How much he lose?"

"About a hundred."

That was nearly half his monthly paycheck. "Who'd he lose to?"

Hastings shrugged. "Me, for one. But the big winner was Stanton. That's who he owed the most to."

"Stanton was there?"

Hastings grinned. "He didn't have no woman that night, I guess, so he sat in on the game. Ryan owed Stanton plenty. We all had to take his IOUs. Nobody liked it, but him bein' the deputy marshal and all — But he paid me back right before I left town."

The woman came over and put some more tar in my cup.

Hastings gazed out the window. "Figure I'll make a little money here and then head back to Arizona. I've got a gal back there."

"Quit reading those dime novels."

He laughed. "Bad influence on me?"

"Definitely. They're a bad influence on everybody who reads them."

He said, "So what happens to you now?"

"Good question. I'll get one of the regional newspapers and see who needs an experienced town marshal. 'Experienced' meaning old."

"You're not old."

"I'm old compared to most men who're town marshals."

"Well, you were young enough to scare the shit out of me, I'll tell you that."

"Well, I'm glad I could do that much for you."

We talked some more, maybe twenty minutes, idle and somewhat strained conversation between strangers, but I was there in body only. I had an idea and it was a terrible idea, an idea I wanted to cut out of my brain with a very sharp knife, but an idea I needed to follow down or it would torment me the rest of my life.

The first place I needed to go was the hotel. I was trying to remember exactly a conversation I'd had with Gunderson. He'd said something that didn't jibe with my memory of things the afternoon Stanton died.

He didn't wake easy. I did everything except start kicking the door in. He'd likely had one of his all-night poker sessions.

He answered in a pair of trousers and an undershirt. And an old Navy Colt that looked as if it could leave quite a hole in anything it was fired at.

"I don't have to talk to you. Get out of here."

The first thing I did was slap him. The second thing I did was grab his wrist and wrench the Colt away. The third thing I did was shove him back inside his room. The poker table he dragged out for a game was covered with cigarette and cigar butts, two empty whiskey bottles, and a pack of playing cards that had photographs of nude women on them.

"You're not the marshal anymore."

"I'm sorry I slapped you." And I was. A couple days of frustration had gone into that slap. There were others I should have used it on first.

My apology seemed to startle him. "What the hell's going on, Morgan? I was asleep."

"I need you to remember something."

"Oh, shit," he said. "You mean about Stanton?"

"Yes."

"It's over, Morgan. In case you hadn't heard, I mean. It was Laura Webley who killed him. I got the word early this morning when the game was still going on."

"I need you to think, Gunderson. Remember something you said to me."

He sighed. He was scarecrow-skinny. He looked tubercular. "All right. What is it?"

"The evening Stanton was killed. You said that Tom Ryan told you that he was up on the second floor looking for Conroy."

"Yeah, Conroy. The con man. That's what he told me."

"You're sure he said Conroy?"

He thought about it. "Pretty sure. Sure as I can recall anyway."

"And what time was this?"

"Right before six."

"How many times did Ryan play cards with you?"

"That isn't any of your business."

"He told you not to tell me about his gambling, didn't he?"

"He's entitled to a personal life, isn't he?"

"How much did he lose altogether playing cards?"

"He's a nice fella, Morgan. I promised I wouldn't tell you."

"How much?"

The sigh again. "You always were a pushy sonofabitch."

"How much, Gunderson?"

"Eight, nine hundred."

"In how long a time?"

He looked miserable. At least betraying a trust made him feel bad. "A couple of weeks."

"You trusted him for that?"

"He said he was coming into some money. Besides, he was a deputy marshal. He could make things bad for me if he wanted to."

"He ever pay you?"

"Yeah, he did. And for what it's worth, he swore off gambling right then and there."

"He paid you after Stanton died, didn't he?"

"Say, what the hell you getting at, Morgan? Ryan didn't kill Stanton. Laura Webley did."

I pitched his gun back to where he sat on the edge of his rumpled bed.

The next two hours went slowly. I ground-tied my horse and waited in the pines on a small hill in back of the place. She played with two of her little girls as she hung laundry in the backyard. She hid in the wind-blown sheets and the two girls would have to find her. Then they'd all laugh and giggle in voices as pure as mountain water.

Just before eleven-thirty she left, one

little girl toddling along on either side of her, a wicker shopping basket hanging from the crook of her elbow. Shopping.

I moved quickly. The inside of the house was a tribute to her industry and frugality. She bought most things second-hand, and yet the place had a hard, stubborn pride about it. There was even a homely beauty to the way the mismatched pieces of furnishings sat next to each other. The cotton curtains were yellow as May sunlight. There was even an old upright piano. She had a nice voice.

Sadly, it didn't take long to find what I was looking for. He'd probably thought that everything would be nice and safe here. Nothing at all to fear. I found a sack for it and carried it back to my horse and stuffed it into my saddlebag.

Then I headed back to town to find the killer.

TWENTY-SIX

He was sitting in my old chair in my old office. Paul Webley was sitting in the chair on the customer side of the desk.

Webley said, "I know a lot of people, Morgan. I can probably find you a job somewhere."

"I appreciate that, Paul. But I guess I'll be staying around here for a while. You never know when my old job just might open up again."

"Now what the hell's that supposed to mean?" Webley said.

I looked at Tom Ryan. He was suddenly gulping, as if swallowing was hard. His eyes started moving this way and that.

"You're saying I can't be here?" Webley said.

"This won't take long," Ryan said. He cleared his throat. "We just need to settle a few things."

Webley seemed to sense the undercurrent here. The eyes narrowed, the jaw muscles bunched. He studied Ryan's face and then he studied mine. "I don't like this."

"I don't much give a shit what you like, Webley. This is between me and Ryan. Now get out."

"You're not the marshal," he said.

"Neither are you."

He got red. Made his face ugly. He was probably thinking of how his old man would've handled this. Brought in some hard boys and pounded on me for a while.

He walked to the door. He walked heavy. He wanted me to know he was somebody important. But I'd known that for too long anyway.

I picked up his Stetson and sailed it to him. "You forgot it."

He cinched it on his head and said, "I'll be up front, Tom, you need anything."

"Thanks, Paul."

I was making a fifty-fifty bet with myself. Whether he'd slam the door or not. He didn't. I owed myself a cup of coffee. But he made up for not slamming the door by walking real heavy down the hall. No spurs. Just loud thudding footsteps like a giant would make.

"I didn't want to say it in front of Webley," I said.

"I'm afraid this is all kind've mysterious to me, Lane."

"Aw, c'mon, Tom. Don't make this any

306

rougher than it needs to be. You might get manslaughter — involuntary, even — if you come up with the right story. He pulled that knife on you and you fought — You know how that one goes. You ought to. You've heard it enough in court."

He went back and sat behind his desk. He put his face in his hands. He started crying. Nothing theatrical. He wasn't good at it. He was embarrassed and he was laughing, too. He took his hands from his face. "God, man, don't ever tell anybody I was crying, all right?"

"You stupid sonofabitch," I said. "You make me feel like crying, too. Tell me you didn't plan to kill him when you went up there."

He reached into his desk drawer and brought out a pint of rye. Then he reached into another desk drawer and brought out two glasses. "I added this since I took over. I have to have a belt every hour or I start shaking so bad people start to notice. And that's no shit. Look at this."

He wasn't kidding. His hand was caught in a spasm.

"You didn't answer my question. You didn't go up there to kill him, did you?"

"Hell, no. I went up there to shake him

down. I was desperate, Lane. I'd been gambling —"

"Yeah, I heard. That was one smart move, Tom. You didn't have enough money worries, you had to start gambling, too?"

"It was my last chance to keep the ranch."

"I really do want to start cryin', Tom. You and that ranch. Everybody told you years ago to get rid of it and move into town and have a nice sensible life for yourself."

He poured us drinks. Shoved mine across to me.

It was the kind of cheap stuff that made you wince, but right then I needed it.

He said, "He was blackmailing Webley, so I thought I'd blackmail *him*. I'd get enough to keep the bank off my back for a while. He was pretty drunk. He came at me with the knife and —"

And that was when the door was flung open inwardly. And there stood everybody's friend Paul Webley. "Don't say another word, Tom."

"What the hell're you doing here?" I said.

"I tiptoed back down the hall. I've heard every word."

"So?" I said.

"So my lawyers will have this dismissed without a trial. Clear self-defense."

Ryan said, "I appreciate the offer, Paul. And it was self-defense. But I just don't want to be beholden to you like that. And anyway, I'm afraid I couldn't do you much good since Lane's going to be marshal again."

"What the hell're you talking about, Tom?" Webley said.

"Grice and the town council — they were talking this morning about asking Lane back. I was out in the hall waiting for the meeting to start. I guess they didn't think I heard." He smiled. "Sort of like you overhearing the two of us, I guess, Paul."

"Well, Morgan sure as hell won't be marshal in this town again. That's something I guarantee you. Guarantee you on the Webley name. A town marshal with wife who used to be —"

I never did find out what he was going to call her. And actually, I didn't much care. I'd been waiting a long, long time to do what I was about to do.

I started it going by clamping my hand over his mouth. And then I said to Ryan, "The judge'll fine me a hundred dollars for this. But I hope you won't put me in a cell until we can go see him."

Ryan grinned. "I guess I can release you on your own recognizance, Lane."

"Thanks, Tom."

And then I did what virtually every man, woman, and child in this valley has wanted to do for years. I hit Paul Webley in the mouth. It was a pretty good punch. Not a great one — I'm not as fast or as muscular as I used to be — but I loosened a couple of teeth and I drew some blood when his lip split. And that was good enough for me.

He started shrieking. It was unmanly as hell, his shrieking, but his rage had made him crazy. Not crazy enough to try and swing on me. But pretty damned crazy nonetheless.

"You know," Ryan said, "you could've hit him harder."

"I know," I said. "Maybe I should've turned that over to a younger fella like you."

He managed to laugh, even given all that was ahead of him. "I sure wish you would've thought of that sooner."

TWENTY-SEVEN

As it turned out, the judge only fined me $25, and the town council picked up the bill for that as a bonus for my becoming town marshal again. A lawyer came in from Denver and said he felt good about a self-defense argument as long as Tom agreed to plead on his attempted extortion charge. That might be some jail time, but not much. He couldn't never be my deputy again, but a couple of factory owners in town gave him standing offers for working as a dock foreman. The ranch is up for sale.

Callie got her teaching job back. There was an angry meeting at which a small band of women argued that she was "unfit" to be around children. But the majority of people at the meeting shouted them down. Decency and common sense — she was a damned good teacher — prevailed. And as you may have figured out by now from your own life, that isn't always the case.

Paul Webley? Nothing happened to him. He could afford the right lawyers and with two of his bought-and-sold flunky judges on the state supreme court, every single charge — including kidnapping — was dropped.

The only satisfaction I get is seeing him on the street occasionally. He scowls and I grin. I grin like hell, as a matter of fact. I consider that a high and true distinction, the only man who ever hit a Webley and lived to tell about it.